the
gentleman
mentor

LESSONS WITH THE DOM BOOK ONE

Kendall Ryan

The Gentleman Mentor
Copyright © 2015 Kendall Ryan

Edited and Formatted by Pam Berehulke, Bulletproof Editing

Cover design and Photography by Sara Eirew

This book is a work of fiction. Names, characters, places, and incidents are either the product of the author's imagination or are used fictitiously.

Chapter One

BRIELLE

Nice, normal girls don't do things like this. They don't hire a man for sex lessons to help them seduce their crush. *What's wrong with me?*

I take another sip of chardonnay and give myself a mental slap on the ass. *Game face, Brie.* Kirby and I would be perfect together, and I know it.

I narrow my eyes at the online ad I came across when browsing the dating sites. It's titled "The Gentleman Mentor," but it's the ad itself that has my heart kicking up speed.

Fit, masculine, educated male, late 20s.
Discreet and forthcoming.

Under my direction and guidance, women learn seduction techniques, how to achieve climax with and without a partner, explore physical gratification, and more.

Dominant, but don't be scared, kitten, I'm not into pain.

Do not be misled. I am pure mischief. But I'm the best kind of trouble.

So, what do you say? Do you feel like being naughty?

If you're ready to reach new levels of pleasure, contact me at @thedominantgentleman. Serious inquiries only.

My pulse pounds in my ears as my cursor hovers over the message link, willing me to do something. Taunting me, mocking me.

I don't know why this is so hard for me. It's a simple message sent from the safety of my own home. I can just throw caution to the wind. If he's a creep or an asshole, which he probably is, I can delete the message and pretend this never happened. And move on with my all-too-depressing life. *Oh, joy.*

I decided to take action after my last date from hell. I'm the poster child for bad first dates. You name it; I've lived it. From online dating disasters where the man who showed up wasn't the guy in the photo, but instead someone's grandfather, to a man whose wife crashed our date and threw a drink in my face. It was a coffee drink too, and freaking hot.

I'm tired of all the games. Especially since Kirby and I would be perfect together, if he'd just get his head out of his ass. After my last bad date, I met up with Kirby for a cocktail since he's my best guy friend. He listened while I complained about men, supplying me with chocolate martinis and his comforting presence.

My take-no-prisoners attitude was born when Kirby, who I'd been secretly in love with for the better part of five years, looked at me solemnly and told me, "Someday I'm going to need to find a good girl like you, Brie, and settle down once and for all."

I wanted to scream, *I'm right here!*

Instead, I nodded and mumbled, "Uh-huh."

Which leads me to tonight. I created a generic profile specifically for this purpose. Fittingly, I'm Bookworm92.

Dear Gentleman Mentor,

As I type the first line, I realize I haven't felt this alive in months. There's something exciting and taboo about this, and apparently that gets my blood pumping. My fingers fly across the keyboard, typing quickly, before I can change my mind. It's like they know something I don't.

I am responding to your ad for lessons in seduction. I'd like your help in attracting a man. A little bit about me—I'm twenty-six, currently single, and I work as a real estate agent. I enjoy reading, yoga, and baking. I guess I'm just a regular girl who needs some extra help. I've never been good at the whole dating thing.

—Potential Client

With my heart pounding out of my chest, my finger hovers over the SEND button. My mouth is bone dry, and my pulse is rioting in my throat. I know this is a big moment, but I can't explain why. I click SEND and take a deep gulp of air.

Leaning against the mountain of pillows piled at my headboard, I allow myself to daydream a little. What if this actually works? I picture myself with Kirby and a fond smile dances on my lips. The advice from my friends is to move on, to find another man who is as passionate about me as I am about him. But the thing is, I've tried. I've been on forty-three first dates and only three second dates. My track record is awful.

How do you even know if you're dating, anyway? It's all texting and meeting up for drinks on neutral ground and then waiting, hoping he'll call. It's casual sex and drunken hookups that you hope lead to more. It's online dating profiles where you try to be witty and charming, and irresistibly sexy and cute. Achieving that perfect combination of girl-next-door and bombshell.

And it's exhausting. I'm not any good at it. I've never been aggressive or flirty, or even very good at making conversation. I'm boring. A bookworm. A dedicated and loyal friend and employee. This is why I need help.

His help.

I glance at my e-mail again and almost shriek when I see his response. I sit up straighter and adjust my laptop screen.

Bookworm92,

Your e-mail bored me to tears. No wonder you need help attracting a man. Tell me about yourself. Hold nothing back. I'm a busy and demanding man. Dig deep. Why are you really single, and what do you need me for? Make me believe it, and I will give you the same candor.

—X

What a prick. I'm about to delete his e-mail and forget the entire failed experiment when a little voice whispers inside me, *He's right.* My e-mail was boring and surface level. It didn't tell him anything about me, or why he should work with me, if he's as busy as his e-mail suggests he is.

I go to my kitchen, pour a shot of vodka, and down it in a single fiery gulp. *Damn, that burns.* I'm not some weak woman who doesn't know what she wants. I let the fire fuel me.

Feeling determined, I return to my bedroom, set my laptop across my legs, and type out a response.

Gentleman Mentor,

> *I've had two sexual partners. Both were long-term relationships. One in college, one after. Jake had a small dick and Drew was decently sized, but didn't know what to do with it. So I guess you could say my sexual experience is lacking.*

I'm height and weight proportionate, and have played sports most of my life, but my small breasts and trim frame make me self-conscious. I'm never going to be described as voluptuous or womanly. I've been told I'm pretty, but I've never felt sexy.

There is a man I'm interested in, a male friend of mine who I've known for five years. I've had a crush on him all that time, but I've never acted on it. Pathetic, huh? But I guess I'm old-fashioned in that I believe a man should make the first move.

I've decided to contact you as a last-ditch effort. It's time for me to let my feelings be known and pursue him, or move on for good. Five years is a long time, and I don't want to waste any more of my life. And, if I'm being honest, the idea of a sexual mentor, a man who knows what he's doing, excites me. Let's just say, I could use the help. It would be reassuring to pursue a man and actually feel like I know

what I'm doing when we got between the
sheets.

Is that honest enough for you? Your turn...

—Bookworm92

His reply comes almost immediately, and I hold my breath while I read it, somehow hoping I've pleased him.

Bookworm92,

Much better, my little bookworm. Your body type is one coveted by many men. You're called a spinner. A petite girl who can be sat down on my cock and used to my liking. You should never feel self-conscious about that.

I think I could help you with a few things, the first of which is self-confidence. Tell me what you want. It is only through open

11

communication and trust that I can take you
there.

—X

A warm shudder passes through me. His message is so blunt, it's almost arrogant. But my body's response is even more intriguing. I've never had a man be quite so direct with me before, and I'm intrigued and slightly frustrated. I have no idea what comes next, but I want to find out.

Gentleman Mentor,

I have no idea how this works, and I feel crazy for even considering it. But I need your help. I want to be better at all of this, attracting someone, the whole dating thing, and sex.

So, what happens now?

—Bookworm92

P.S. I noticed your ad said that you're a Dominant, and while I don't know much about it, it does make me a little nervous. Plus, I'm not a submissive, so...?

A small ding signals his quick reply.

Bookworm92,

You're not crazy. I applaud you for taking the first step in contacting me. It shows me how dedicated you are. You're demonstrating your willingness to learn and in turn, proving your dedication to succeeding. I'm not looking for a weekend fuck. I can get that at any corner bar. I take my work seriously, and I would expect you to do the same.

Regarding my dominant nature—when you hire me to be your mentor, I am in charge. I decide your lessons, your rewards, and your punishments. There will be no negotiation,

13

which is why it's very important that I learn your goals, fears, desires, and hard limits.

It takes an incredible amount of courage to submit, and I'm aware that you're putting your faith in me. Despite how direct all this may seem, I live up to the word "gentleman" in my e-mail. You will be safe with me and treated with firm respect.

However, your boundaries will be pushed, limits tested, and the woman who emerges will know more about who she is and what she can offer a partner. You may not think you are a submissive, but contacting me for help is quite telling, yes? You're willing to put yourself aside and let me take the lead. That's good enough for me.

I've done this many times, and I can likely anticipate what some of your questions might be. We can cover those at our first session.

The next step is to meet in person and make sure this will work for us both. In the meantime, tell me one thing you're scared of— what you think is holding you back. And also your schedule. I'm fairly open next week—I'm free on both Thursday evening and Sunday afternoon.

Speak soon,

—X

I stare blankly at his response. While I appreciate his lengthy e-mail—which helps me understand a lot more, both about this process and him being a Dom—doubt creeps into my mind. I have only a general idea of BDSM, and it's not something I've ever felt the urge to explore. Honestly, I don't know if I can do this.

I read his words again. He's going to explore and learn my deepest fears and desires. He's asking too much and I don't even know him, so how can I be expected to share these most intimate parts of me?

A bubble of laughter rises up my throat at the irony. I'll be sharing a lot more of my intimate parts with him if I pursue this.

I close my computer and pace my bedroom, realizing I'm stressed out and I haven't even met the guy yet. Pulling a deep breath into my lungs, I decide I'll sleep on it. I'll wait a day or two to respond, give myself time to think about this. Having made that one small decision, I immediately feel better.

I head into the bathroom. Turning the faucet to hot, I let the tub fill. Sinking down into water that's almost too warm, I sigh deeply. With my eyes closed and my body in a state of relaxation, I let my mind wander.

Almost immediately, I picture Kirby. With his broad shoulders, messy blond hair, and striking blue eyes, he is my warmth. My comfort blanket. He has been for a long time. He's been a constant in my life, the man who has supported me emotionally through many ups and downs, loaning me money after graduation when the real estate market dropped, helping me move into my first apartment, and sending me my favorite flowers—peonies—on my birthday every year.

With a newfound sense of purpose, I rise from the tub, suddenly feeling silly for questioning myself. I don't want to miss my only shot at getting actual help. This arrangement with the Gentleman Mentor— whoever he is—may be unconventional, but it might be just the thing I need to help move me from friend zone to girlfriend material where Kirby is concerned. And I'd be lying if I didn't admit that e-mailing back and forth with my mentor has me feeling intrigued and slightly turned on.

Tossing on my cotton robe, I head for my laptop and open my e-mail. Glancing at his last message, I recall that he's asked what I'm most scared of, along with my schedule. I fidget for a few minutes before typing out a hasty response, leaving out the part I don't know how to answer.

Gentleman Mentor,

I would prefer to meet on Thursday. I'm supposed to go to my parents' house on Sunday, and if I have to miss it, I don't want my mom asking why. ;)

But can I ask you something? Has a woman ever backed out after meeting you in person?

—Bookworm92

Bookworm92,

Thursday would be fine. And no, a woman has never backed out after meeting me.

—X

I read his message with a growing sense of comfort. That's good to know. Perhaps it's simple curiosity because I have no idea what he looks like, but I'm afraid that he's unattractive. I haven't seen a picture after all. I know it's terribly shallow, but I couldn't go through with it if I'm not attracted to him.

Another thought flits through my brain and my nerves are back. My next e-mail flies from my fingers.

Have you ever refused services after meeting a woman?

His reply comes right away.

Bookworm92,

Yes, twice.

—X

I read his message and worry that he could refuse me if he doesn't like what he sees. It's not a comforting thought. I chew on my lip, unsure what to write back next when another message comes through. It's as if he knows I'm hesitating and takes the decision from my hands.

Bookworm92,

> *We will meet Thursday at 8 p.m. at the Dakota. You will order one drink and wait for me at the bar. Dress in all black, wear something sexy, and underneath, your panties and bra will be red.*

—X

Chapter Two

BRIELLE

"You'll call me the second you're done, right?" my best friend, Julie, pleads through the phone.

"I'll call you," I promise for the seventeenth time. "Unless I end up chopped up into little bits and tossed into a garbage can. In that case, you'll hear about it on the eleven o'clock news."

"I thought you were meeting in a public place?" she asks, her tone worried.

"Yes, we are. He said to meet him at a place called the Dakota. But a girl can never be too careful."

"The jazz club downtown?"

"That's the one." I'd never heard of it, so I researched it online. "I'm pulling in now. I've gotta go."

"Call. Me. Immediately. After," she orders.

Rolling my eyes at her overzealous tone, I promise her again. "The minute I'm done."

I pull into a parking spot near the entrance and cut the engine on my practical sedan. Glancing up into the rearview mirror, I meet my own eyes and giggle.

Julie's excitement is totally warranted. Normally we are both so calm and levelheaded, this is by far the craziest thing either of us has ever done. I'm glad she's sharing in my excitement over this plan. Then again, I'm just happy to have my buddy system in place—someone ready to dial the authorities if I turn up missing. It's not a comforting thought, and my belly tenses.

Without the radio or Julie's voice in my ear, the interior of my car is silent, all except for my pounding heart. *God, this is truly crazy, isn't it?*

I flip down my visor to check my hair and makeup in the mirror. I took extra time and care this morning getting ready, straightening my hair until the glossy brown tresses fell in a long, straight line down my back, choosing my black sweater dress and knee-high boots with tights, wearing all black just like he instructed, and applying light makeup.

But now, it's almost six o'clock, and after shuffling around the snowy Chicago streets and showing apartments and homes to eager couples all day, I look every bit as tired as I feel. I dab a bit of powder under my eyes, hoping to brighten my complexion, and reapply soft pink lipstick.

Once done, I smile at my reflection. I look marginally better.

I can't believe how fast the week went by, that it's somehow Thursday already. I had no further communication with the Gentleman Mentor all week, other than an e-mail he sent last night when he confirmed our appointment and the location.

Seeing that I only have five minutes until our meeting, I grab my purse and exit the car. I want to be inside and seated at the bar as he instructed before he arrives. Striding across the parking lot, I notice the sky is painted in pink and orange hues at that point just before the sun sets.

It's pretty and romantic, I think, then correct myself with a shake of my head.

This isn't romance. It's business. I have to keep my head clear.

Chapter Three

HALE

There's a certain energy that runs through my veins the first time I meet a new client. Tonight is no different. On the outside, I'm collected and calm, but inside, I'm filled with anticipation.

I've never brought a woman so close to my home turf, but of course my little bookworm has no way of knowing the underground BDSM club, Crave, I hold a membership to is located directly next door to the jazz club where she should be arriving at any minute. I can practically smell the fear and excitement on her skin.

From an armchair near the fireplace, I watch the scene playing out in front of me—a woman strapped to a leather bench while a Domme teases her, trailing a flogger along the back of her thighs.

I watch the women with mild interest. Floggers and whips aren't my thing. I prefer my own two hands. There's nothing quite as satisfying as the crack of my flesh against hers, the feel of heat radiating from warmed skin. As I watch her squirm and try to be quiet, I appreciate the amount of courage her public submission takes.

From across the room I see Reece, and based on the look of satisfaction on his face, I'd guess he's returning from one of the private rooms. He's the owner of the club, but so laid-back, most people wouldn't suspect that.

I've visited a couple of other clubs, and Reece's club is by far the best. The others felt cold and more like a gymnasium, with sterile equipment and wide-open spaces, yet this place feels dark, moody, and sensual. The play spaces are built for quiet, sensuous scenes, leaving the more risqué kinks for the private rooms. Sconces provide dim lighting and low bass-filled beats thrum in the background, creating a soft hum of anticipation. There's no wonder it's grown into the biggest fetish club in Chicago in three short years.

When Reece gets closer, I tip my head in silent greeting. The big man lumbers up, squinting at me curiously. "Cameron *Fucking* Hale. I haven't seen you in, what…at least a month, brother?"

"Sounds about right." I cross my arms over my chest, feeling oddly defensive. This lifestyle is lived out differently for each person in it, but Reece doesn't seem to get that. He doesn't understand why I'm not here every night enjoying a different sub.

I'm really not one for a meet-n-fuck. Sure, I've done it before, when necessity calls for it, but I much prefer the slow, sensual exploration of a partner's naughtiest desires, and then exploit the fuck out of them. Pushing a woman to her limit is as gratifying to me as the sexual release itself.

Reece takes the seat next to me and surveys the room with the watchful eye of a predator. He's a businessman and a Dom in all aspects—qualities I appreciate and can relate to. I silently note the scene in front of us has progressed to nipple clamps and ice cubes. *Interesting.*

"Where have you been, man?" he asks. "I've missed seeing your pretty face."

I shrug. "Working. Staying busy." He knows as a senior associate at the law firm, intent on making partner, I work way too fucking many hours.

He turns to me with a smug grin. "Still working to train the uncivilized?"

"I'm still mentoring, yes. But trust me, I get a lot out of it."

His smile says he's not so sure. "Yes, you were always that way—a do-gooder. I like them well-trained and ready to play. I'll show them my preferences, break any bad habits their previous Dom taught them. But, shit, I don't want to start from scratch."

I know what he means; a well-trained sub is a beautiful thing. Still, something excites me about taking a woman to that place. The journey is sometimes more gratifying than the destination.

"It's more fun than you might think." My thoughts drift to my newest conquest, and my heart rate kicks up a notch. Glancing at my watch, I see it's just now six. My nervous little kitten is probably entering the club next door, heart pounding and eyes wide. Imagining the fear and uncertainty swimming inside her arouses me.

"You too busy for lunch next week?" Reece asks, his eyes still on the women before us. "It's been too long."

"Never too busy for lunch. Just come downtown to my office."

"Sounds good, man." He claps me once on the back.

Reece, despite not understanding my preferences and tastes, is the closest thing I have to a best friend. I have work acquaintances, friends, and even a roommate, but none of them know about my lifestyle. Reece knows all about my past and supported me through the shittiest time of my life. He's the one who introduced me to this life.

"I have an appointment to get to," I say, rising to my feet. "But I'll see you next week?"

"Count on it. I'll need to hear all about your newest plaything." He grins at me unevenly.

"Not a chance. You know I don't kiss and tell, like you."

"Or spank and tell." He smiles again. "Have fun tonight."

"I always do," I say, tipping my head before heading to the door.

Immediately upon entering, I congratulate myself on choosing the Dakota. It's perfect, swamped with a sexually-charged energy. Moody jazz floats through the air, and dim lighting casts faint shadows in all the corners.

When I spot her, my stride falters. But only for a second. *Holy fucking hell.* Anyone watching wouldn't know my entire world just got knocked on its ass. I'm not usually one for keeping secrets, yet the moment I see her, I know what must be done.

Fixing a cool expression on my face, I start toward her again.

She hasn't noticed me yet, so I take a moment to drink her in. Her cocktail is half full, and her hand is gripping the glass. She's nervous. And questioning herself. She takes another sip and her shoulders relax.

Good girl.

I approach her from the side of the bar—and with her eyes trained on the front door, it's not the direction she's expecting.

"Bookworm?" I ask, though I know it's her. I can smell the scent of nervousness and desire on her.

She turns to face me, her expression a puzzle. "Yes," she says softly after several tense moments.

I take a minute to survey her. She's petite, just like I imagined her. Brunette. Big blue eyes whose gaze drifts between mine and the floor as if she doesn't know where to look. There must be some goddamn mistake, because there's no way she'd need any help attracting a man. But if it's my help she wants, I won't refuse her.

"May I?" I ask, pulling out the seat next to her and moving toward it. She's timid, and I need to remember my manners.

"Please," she says. "I'm Brielle."

"No names."

"Everyone calls me Brie, though." She twists her hands in her lap.

"Sweetheart?" I say, and her gaze darts up to mine. "I said no names."

"Oh. I'm sorry." She swallows down her nerves. "But what should I call you?"

"You may call me Dom."

Our gazes connect, and a flash of desire pools low in my spine. *Fucking hell.* This should be interesting.

Chapter Four

BRIELLE

"You want to be fucked hard. Taken and worshiped. Am I right?" he asks, pinning me with that dark, sexy stare. It's as if he's reaching into my mind and determining my wants, needs, and filthiest desires before I even speak them.

I lift my glass to my lips before realizing it's empty. *Crap.*

He's moved us over to a booth in the dark corner of the club where he can watch me and all my embarrassing reactions to his intrusive questions without interruption.

"Answer me," he says. His tone is firm, yet kind, and his eyes haven't left mine for a second.

A hot shiver runs through me. "Y-yes," I manage.

My first impression of him is that he is tall. Much taller than me, with a mess of dark hair and the most gorgeous mocha-colored eyes that have flecks of chocolate and caramel. His square jawline screams of masculinity, yet his full lips suggest a softness to him. Nicely sculpted muscles under a finely tailored black suit. Expensive wristwatch. A couple of days' worth of beard growth on his jaw. Notes of crisp cologne greeted me when he neared, causing my heart to riot.

My second impression, with his commanding tone that demands attention and his direct nature, is that he enjoys being in control. Though, I suppose that's no surprise. *News flash, Brie—he's a Dom!*

He's handsome, completely gorgeous, and I'm both relieved and nervous. I wonder what he thinks of me.

"Your hands are shaking," he says. "Tell me why."

I look down at my hands resting on the table. He's right. I can see a slight tremble in the tips of my fingers. "I guess I'm a little nervous. I've never done this type of thing before."

He nods once, still scrutinizing me. "Are you sure that's all? Have you eaten?"

I open my mouth to respond when I realize that I really haven't. Three cups of coffee and a muffin ten hours ago probably don't count.

"N-no." I hate how I keep stumbling over my words, but I can honestly say I've never been quite so thrown off in the presence of a man. I was too nervous to eat lunch and assumed I'd eat dinner when I got back to my apartment tonight.

He lifts his hand and signals to the waitress. She strides over a second later carrying two menus. Dom refuses his but hands one to me, then dismisses our waitress.

I sit there, holding the menu and feeling like an idiot. "I'm not ordering and eating if you're not."

"I'm not the one shaking from lack of food."

"You can't be serious. I'm fine." I place the menu on the table and move my hands to my lap so he can't see them.

He leans closer, his eyes pinned on mine. "Lesson one. You need to put yourself first, Brielle. You need to take better care of yourself if you expect someone else to."

My name on his lips surprises me. He said no names, yet he didn't hesitate to use it. "You can just call me Brie," I remind him. "Everyone else does."

"I'm not everyone else. And it's a beautiful name."

My skin warms at his compliment. "It's a mouthful. I think it was my parents' compromise between Brianna and Gabrielle. But honestly, don't worry, I'm fine," I add, brushing off his concern.

"I need you to understand something. When you are in my care, I'm responsible for you. I need you to trust me to care for you. And right now, I would like you to have something to eat."

I nod. He's abrupt and controlling, but I can't argue that his intentions aren't sincere. I pick up the menu again and scan the pages for something that sounds appealing, but food is the last thing on my mind. I see a field-green salad and close my menu just as the waitress approaches again.

"Yes, the field-green salad please," I say confidently. I want to prove to him that I'm not a complete moron. I can feed myself, for fuck's sake.

His brows draw together as he watches me. "Are you a vegetarian?"

"No."

He turns to the waitress. "Can you add chicken or steak to that salad?"

"Yes, either," she says, looking between the two of us as if she's trying to figure out what's going on.

He turns to me once again. "You should have protein, Brielle. It will make you feel better."

Now that he knows my name, it seems he's taking every opportunity to use it. *The bastard.* "Chicken, please," I say to the waitress, my humiliation complete.

"Would you like another drink?" His voice is low as if he's trying to spare my embarrassment. The concern in his eyes is genuine.

"Yes, please."

"What are you having?" the server asks.

"Peach schnapps with soda," I say.

"That'll be all," he says to the waitress, taking the menu from my hands and handing it to her.

When my salad arrives, he watches me while I eat, his mouth curling into a slight smile when I take a bite of chicken. This man is strange. Why would he care if I ate? I just met him. And I'm certainly not at risk of starving to death.

Realizing I've eaten almost every bite without offering him any makes me self-conscious. There's a ripe cherry tomato left at the edge of the plate.

"Would you like a tomato?" I ask.

"No, I don't want your tomato. At least, not in the sense you're offering." He smirks.

My cheeks burn, but I pretend not to notice his cheeky remark. Instead, I take my last bite of salad, wipe my mouth on the napkin, and look up at him. I'm ready to get down to business.

"If we decide to work together, how does it work?" I take a sip of my cocktail and wait for him to answer.

"We'll get to that, but first you failed to answer my last question in our e-mail exchange."

I blink at him, feigning ignorance.

"What is one thing you're scared of?" he says to remind me.

I swallow and take a deep gulp of air. I've taken several days to consider his question, somehow knowing that he wouldn't let me get away without answering.

"My greatest desire is to be loved, and I'm most afraid of never finding it," I say softly. It sounds silly, overly romantic, and immature when I say it out loud, but it's the absolute truth.

His next words are sharp and blunt. "Don't be afraid of what you want. I can turn you into a sex goddess that men want to fuck, and I can make you into the perfect housewife. My goal is to learn *you* and help you reach your goals."

"I just want a certain man to notice me," I say quietly.

"I understand."

I look down at the empty plate in front of me. My stomach is turning somersaults, and the salad I ate is threatening to return.

"You're nervous." His voice is soft and controlled.

"Yes," I admit.

"And you're unsure about working with me."

"I need a little time to think it all over."

He nods once in understanding. "The choice is yours. I get thirty of those e-mails a day. If you're not sure, if you can't devote yourself to this one hundred percent, then I'm afraid I can't either. I'm a busy man, and I only have time for serious students, Brielle."

I take a moment to mull it over. Although I need the help, there's something that still confuses me. "This dominant thing...I'm not sure about that since I'm not a submissive. I don't know how this will work." *And I really don't see how being tied up and spanked will achieve anything.*

"If I told you to go into the restroom and remove your panties right now…does that excite you?"

My pulse throbs in my neck, and my belly stirs with butterflies. "Maybe a little."

"That's what I thought. Don't worry about the labels. I'm your guide, your leader on this journey. Are you okay with that?"

"I guess so."

"Yes or no, Brielle?"

"Yes," I manage.

"Good."

"How do we begin?" My voice is shaky, but at least I'm able to maintain eye contact with the gorgeous and domineering man before me.

"We would meet weekly at a time and place I choose. I would issue you a challenge. As I get to know you and see how you react to me, I will know which things you need help with. My tutoring would

41

center on those issues. You have to give yourself to me fully and trust in this process for it to work. For you, it would likely be self-confidence, the art of seduction, and as you've indicated, sexual awareness."

Everything he's just described is exactly what I want, what I crave. There's only one thing that's bugging me… "You don't really expect me to call you *Dom*, do you?"

He watches me curiously. "I do."

I'm desperate to know his name, and I don't even know why. Maybe because this isn't some game to me. This is my life. And if I'm trusting this stranger with my body—and my head—I want to know more about who he is.

"You already know my name. Why can't you just tell me your first name?"

He lets out a heavy sigh, and I can tell there's something he dislikes about me questioning him. "I've had two unfortunate incidents of women falling for me and trying to track me down in my personal life. My first name is uncommon, and because of what's happened in the past, I can't risk it. Or rather, I won't. So it's Dom or nothing. Your call."

"Are you married?"

"No."

"A girlfriend?"

"No." His tone is firm, and even though I don't know if I should, I believe him.

"You'll need to sign a basic nondisclosure agreement. Anything we do together shouldn't be shared or discussed with outside parties—that's to protect us both. I also insist that clients have STD testing completed. The results take about a week to come back, which is fine. Our first meeting isn't going to be sexual."

"It's not?" I hate the sound of disappointment in my voice. *Where the hell did that come from?*

"Is that a problem?" His mouth curves into a slight grin as if he's just read my mind and liked what he saw.

I straighten my spine. "Of course not."

x

43

"For you, and what we hope to accomplish together, I would recommend six sessions. It's enough for me to give you the time and attention you deserve, but not so much time together that..." He trails off, losing some of his self-assuredness for the first time this evening.

"Not so much time together that, what?" I ask.

"I don't like to do more sessions than that because women tend to get attached to me."

I laugh despite his serious expression. There's no way I'll get attached to him. I'm still trying to wrap my head around how being with a Dom will work, even for this short period, and have no interest in pursuing that lifestyle long term.

"You can take some time to think about it. I know for some it's expensive—"

"I want to do it," I blurt.

"Okay then. I'll e-mail you the nondisclosure documents, a few local clinics that offer STD testing, and the pricing sheet for my services."

"I understand." Nothing worthwhile is free, and I'm prepared to pay for his help. I can tell in our one short conversation that he is the real deal. As nice as it is to have a savings account, the money is doing me no good just sitting there. This is about me taking charge of my life and going after what I want. And right now, I want this unabashed man to teach me what he knows.

"I want you to make a list of all the sexual things you've wanted to try, but never been brave enough to ask for."

"I—okay." The idea of the task makes me a little uncomfortable, but maybe that's the idea. I'm here to grow. To learn.

"We need to delve into your past. Specifically, have you ever pleasured yourself? If so, how, when, the frequency, et cetera. I will need you to describe in detail a couple of fantasies. I want to understand your wants and desires, Brielle. It's the only way I can help you."

I take a deep breath. I understand now, watching him, he doesn't just want inside my body, he wants inside my head. It's a big leap of faith on my part.

"All right," I whisper.

He leans closer, his mouth twitching with a smile. "Do you touch yourself?"

My breath lodges in my throat. He wants me to answer *now*? I thought he meant later—through the anonymity of e-mail. "S-sometimes."

"With a toy or with your fingers in your pussy?" He leans closer, close enough that I can smell his expensive cologne.

I had a toy, but it broke from overuse. Somehow, I'm sure that would only make him laugh. "With my fingers," I whisper.

He reaches across the table and lifts my hand, studying it. Soulful jazz floats through the air, creating a sexy atmospheric pressure all around us as the gorgeous singer's voice flirts with us from across the room. Hot and bothered in a way I've never experienced, I realize I'm flushed and warm from head to toe.

"You have small, delicate fingers." His finger glides along my index and middle fingers, inspecting me and tickling my skin with his light touch. "It will feel much different when I fuck you with my hand, but you'll tell me everything you like and how to make you come. Won't you, Brielle?"

I swallow. "Yes." My voice is a tiny whisper, and I know my cheeks are bright red.

"And what about limits? Is there anything you'd rather not try?"

He's right; I have to take control of my life, my sex life included, if I want to succeed. I'm determined to be confident in this exchange.

My eyes meet his. "Oral sex."

He makes a small sound of surprise in his throat. "Tell me why."

"My gag reflex—" I stop myself. I don't want to sound like an idiot to someone who's obviously much more sexually experienced than me. I don't want him to know that I gagged and sputtered like an idiot the first and last time I tried it. "It's just not something I enjoy."

He leans close, his voice dropping low, and his entire presence dominates every inch of my personal space. My inner muscles clench.

"I can teach you how to suck cock like a fucking pro. How to deep-throat so well that no man will ever leave your bed. Would you like that, Brielle, my cock buried deep in your throat while my voice coaches you through? My thick shaft pumping in and out of your mouth while my hands massage your throat until you relax and take me?"

Between my thighs grows damp, and I drop my gaze from his to the table. It's too intense between us. God, we've only just met. Surely he understands I can't go from zero to dirty talk in thirty minutes? The best I can do is to mumble unintelligible replies.

I nod. "I could try, if you wanted me to."

His mouth curls into a devilish grin. "Are you wet, peach?" he asks, out of the blue.

Dear God, it's like this man can read my mind. I need a better poker face if I hope to survive my encounters with him.

As I look down, averting my eyes, I hear him chuckle softly. My reticence is the only answer he needs.

Chapter Five

HALE

Her responses have all been perfect in their delicate submission. The slight dip of her chin, the lowering of her eyes, the pink flush of her cheeks at my vulgar language. Things are going better than anticipated, and I'm a happy man at the moment, though my expression remains cool and neutral, so as not to give anything away.

I pushed her to make a decision, told her that I had droves of women waiting in line, which is true, but I'd clear my schedule in a heartbeat for the chance to work with her. There's something about her that draws me in, makes me want a taste of the sweet submission she has buried away.

"Aren't you going to order a drink?" she asks, noting the plain water in front of me.

I rarely drink alcohol; I don't like to give up control. But this beautiful creature before me doesn't need to know such a personal detail. "I'm fine. Is there anything else you want to know?"

She nods, and a little crease appears between her brows while she thinks about what to ask me. "Why do you do this? This mentoring thing?"

"You want to know if I'm a normal guy and what I get out of this, right?"

She nods. "Yes, basically."

I tilt my head to the side, considering her quizzical look. "Trust me, it's a question I get often. I understand."

I take a moment, glancing around at our surroundings before responding. Even for men not involved in the lifestyle, I've found that by and large, men are attracted to women who are able to submit. Not weak, timid women without opinions and original thought. No, we want a strong woman who can match our wit, intellect, and stamina in and out of the bedroom. A woman who is confident enough in herself and her sexuality that she's not afraid to leave her ego at the door and let me push all her boundaries. A woman who will drop to her knees at my command and trust me to handle every detail. I find that sexy as fuck. And that's what I aim to teach the women I mentor.

"I have a high-powered, stressful corporate job. I found BDSM a few years ago, and it felt like home." I won't tell her about the personal tragedy that led me there. "Many Doms have a single sub—a partner to explore this lifestyle with, and since I haven't found that one right fit yet, this is my way of staying active in the community. And, honestly, I enjoy teaching. It's very gratifying to me to see a woman reach her potential, to watch her let go of all her insecurities and blossom under my guidance."

Brielle looks at me with a sort of awe. "That's beautiful, actually," she says, surprising the shit out of me. I'm no saint; I teach women how to fuck like porn stars for my own personal benefit, as well as their own, but I nod at the compliment.

"Tell me something about this man you want to win over."

A smile transforms her face, and she lets out a happy little sigh. "Kirby is..." She slaps a hand over her mouth. "Sorry. No names. He's been my best guy friend for about five years now. We met in college and have always been just friends. He's sweet and thoughtful and kind, everything I want in a man."

"What does he do? Professional-type job, or something with his hands?"

She stifles a laugh. "Kirby? Do something with his hands? God, no. He's a lawyer."

Feeling nauseated, I nod. "Got it." I don't need to know much about her Prince Charming, only that he's male and straight. After I'm done with her, the dickhead won't be able to resist her.

"You said you'd be able to anticipate questions I might have."

I nod.

"I want to see how good you are." She smirks as if she's waiting for me to enlighten her.

"I'm the best. Don't doubt that for a second."

She chews on her lip and lets the silence engulf us before continuing.

Watching her, I realize there's something I'm enjoying about her reactions, and there's no reason to rush this. I'll just be heading home alone to an empty house after, or perhaps stopping and paying a visit to Chrissy if I'm in the mood.

"You've been wondering what type of women generally come to me for help."

She smirks. "Yes, actually."

I nod. *I told you I'm the fucking best.*

"They're regular women. Your girlfriends, coworkers, and acquaintances. They are women who never reached orgasm. Women whose partner has strayed, and they want to learn how to satisfy their man, women who want to take control of their lives."

She nods along as I speak, seemingly enchanted by my words. Although there have been a few times when a woman has requested my help in winning over a man she already knows, like Brielle, I don't tell her that. I've never seen this scenario successfully play out. If a man hasn't taken notice, there's a reason. There is truth in that old saying, "He's just not that into you." If he were, you wouldn't be in my bed.

But I won't burst her pretty little bubble today. Because something tells me it would be fun to see her ride my dick and learn to be the seductress I see lurking inside her.

Chapter Six

BRIELLE

I'm lost in his eyes, in his deep, watchful stare, wondering what will happen next. He's in no hurry to rush our first meeting, and I appreciate that. This is all so new for me; I want to soak up every detail.

"Did you do what I asked?" His voice is soft and controlled. It's the kind of voice that washes over you, making you feel warm and desirable. I could listen to him speak for hours.

"What do you mean?" My heart begins to hammer as if it knows something I don't.

He leans in closer, and my pulse pounds in my ears as he draws near. His gaze never wavers. Never strays from mine. Being in his presence is overwhelming. He's so strong and sure, as I suppose a Dom is, but I had no idea it would feel like *this*.

My body heats up, growing warm for him. He hasn't even touched me, hasn't spoken a single word. He simply studies me from across the table, and it's as if he owns me. He could do anything he wanted, and I'd mold to his wishes.

His eyes remain on mine, and though my natural response is to look away, I don't. This is a test, and one that I very much want to pass. It's as though he can read me with a single look. Those warm, mocha-colored eyes just dismantled me like a bomb.

"Your panties," he says coolly after several minutes. "Go into the bathroom and take them off. Place them into your purse and bring them to me."

Say what now?

In his e-mail he asked me to wear red panties, and it was a point I fought with myself over. I didn't own a red panty-and-bra set. And I knew he'd never see them anyway—this being the first time we've met, and my general sense of modesty. So why, for the love of God, I rushed out to Victoria's Secret at the last minute last night and bought a red G-string and push-up bra, I can't explain. Maybe my subconscious anticipated this moment.

"I can't just go take off my panties in a public restroom." I meet his icy stare with an incredulous look of my own.

He raises his chin. "The choice is yours. I need to know you're dedicated to this. To me."

This is apparently my first test. And my stupid type-A personality not only wants to pass, I want to ace it.

I rise from the table on shaky legs. He watches me while I lift my purse from the seat beside me and exit the booth. I feel wicked and dangerous, and suppress a naughty giggle at the thought. I like this side of me that so rarely comes out to play. This feeling could become addictive.

When I enter the ladies' room, I glance into the mirror to see a smirk slashed across my face. My cheeks are stained with two splotches of pink, and there's a mischievous glint in my eyes. We've hardly begun working together, and I feel like a different woman already. Funny how taking control of your life will do that to you.

Alone in the bathroom, I slip into the first stall and latch the door behind me. A moment later, the outer door opens and two sets of high-heeled shoes click across the tile floor.

"Did you see who that was? He was sitting with a woman, but now he's alone," a woman's voice says.

"How could I miss him? Six foot three of sexy with a bedroom stare powerful enough to knock you up from across the room," the second woman answers, and they share a wave of polite laughter.

I can't explain how I know, but I'm sure they're talking about my date. With my skirt bunched up around my hips, I wait and listen.

"It's good to see him out. That was so sad what happened to him."

"It was devastating," the second woman agrees.

The water from the faucet drowns out their voices and I can't make out their words, but I'm trembling. They implied that something tragic happened to him, and now that I think about it, there has to be more to his story.

He's a handsome, successful bachelor. Why is he single? Why does he do this?

Unease churns inside me. I'm not sure if it's wise to get involved in something I don't understand. But what choice do I have? The thought of returning to my lonely single existence sounds miserable. Tonight is the most successful date I've had in a long time. Sure, it's probably just because I'm paying him, but still, I feel different. Calmer, more graceful, in control.

When the women exit the bathroom, I force myself back into the present. There's no way I'm giving up now. I need to see what happens next. I push my fingers into the strings at my hips and slide the panties down my thighs. Depositing the tiny scrap of red lace into my purse, I exit the restroom with my shoulders squared.

In my absence, the waitress has removed my salad plate and our glasses, and left the check. I slide back into my spot in the booth, sitting directly across from him. His mouth twitches with a smile as if he wants to ask me how it went, but he remains ever silent and watchful. It's as if he *knows* I'm moments away from handing over the evidence, and doesn't need to fill the silence with senseless chatter. His confidence is addictive.

I match his self-assured posture and reach inside my small black handbag, balling the panties in my fist. Swallowing a sudden blip of nerves, I reach across the table, extending my hand toward him. Discreetly, he reaches out and takes my offering, immediately moving his hand to his jacket pocket and placing them safely inside.

He's going to keep them? I figured this was an assessment, designed to make sure I could follow basic instructions. I didn't imagine him pocketing my underwear to inspect later.

Geez.

"If there's nothing else, I suppose we're finished for tonight," he says, watching me coolly.

My head is clouded by what I overheard in the restroom and I'm desperate for answers. Unsure what else to do, I nod my consent.

He stands and watches as I grab my purse and exit the booth. He insisted on paying the bill, which was generous, considering all he had was water, and I had cocktails as well as a meal.

When we reach the front of the jazz club, he holds the door and I step out into the night. The crisp Chicago fall demands to be noticed, and I wrap my arms around myself, wondering why I hadn't worn a coat.

"Will you be okay getting home?" he asks.

"I'll be fine. I don't live too far." I hardly touched my second drink, and the buzz I had has worn off.

Lifting my hand to his mouth, he presses a kiss to the back of it. The gesture is so unexpected, so intimate, that I flinch.

His eyes flash on mine, noting my uneasiness. "I need you to be comfortable with me, Brielle," he says in a low voice, his mouth still on my hand.

I nod. "I know. This is just all so new to me."

"How long has it been since you've been intimate with a man?" he asks, studying me.

I consider lying, because, damn, the truth is embarrassing. But he's been honest with me in everything so far, at least I think he has, so I decide to treat him with the same courtesy. "Four years."

His throat works up and down, the only indication of his surprise. "I promise I will make it good for you. You have nothing to be scared of. We'll decide on a safe word, and all play will stop when you use it. Do you understand?"

"Yes." I blink up at him, fighting off the shiver tickling my spine.

"What else is bothering you?"

His ability to read me like a book, despite us having just met, is staggering. "It's just that I'm not used to a man paying me such focused attention, and you're a very attractive man, and you said women have gotten attached to you, and I don't want that to happen."

Oh God, I'm babbling. *Someone shut me up! Was there truth serum in that second drink?*

His mouth draws into a tight line. "That would be a very bad idea."

I swallow and nod.

He draws closer, and I can smell mint on his breath. "I know you think this is about Kirby, but this is about *you*. I'm going to help you become the woman you want to be. One that no man can resist."

He's right. That's what I want, regardless of what happens with Kirby. I'm tired of dating dickheads. I want a shot with a good guy, and if it's not meant to be with Kirby, well, then at least the Gentleman Mentor will have taught me some new tricks for winning over my real Mr. Right. I deserve love, and I will work hard to make it happen.

"You have to trust me. Trust in this process. It's going to be fun, I promise." He gives me a flirty wink and treats me to that dazzling white smile.

Dizzy, I'm not sure how to respond.

"What have you got to lose?" He leans close, his mouth almost at my neck. My impulse is to lean into him, to give him everything he wants, but that makes no sense. I hardly know him.

His lips brush against my throat. They're warm and soft, and I can tell he's restraining himself from pressing me further.

Pulling back, he straightens his jacket. "Good night, Brielle."

"Night," I murmur, transfixed by him. I try to think of something witty to say, some comment about my panties that are still in his jacket pocket, but I'm at a loss.

He doesn't say anything else, almost as if he wants the anticipation to build between us. It's apparent that he's intentional in everything he does, and this moment is no exception. He waits while I get into my car before walking over to a black luxury sedan and climbing inside.

• • •

HALE

That was interesting as fuck. When I walked in and saw her, I thought it was a dream. I vowed then and there to treat her as any other client, because if the truth came out, it would ruin everything I've built for myself.

I watch her car pull away and wait until her taillights disappear from sight. Then I reach into my jacket pocket and remove the tiniest piece of red lace I've ever seen. These are a sore excuse for panties. I ought to punish her, spank her fine ass for torturing me with the knowledge that she barely kept her pussy covered all day while waiting to meet me. Was she trying to tease me? That won't do. I can't have her thinking she has the upper hand. I need to show her who's in charge.

I bring the fabric to my nose and inhale deeply. Sweet feminine arousal greets me. *Fucking hell.* My cock hardens and tugs at my zipper. Glancing down, damn if I don't see a tiny damp spot in her panties. Something tells me my new little sub is going to be fun to play with.

But in the meantime, I start my car and head toward Chrissy's apartment.

Chapter Seven

BRIELLE

I can't even put into words what just happened. I ate a meal at the command of a man I didn't know, responded as he peppered me with erotic questions, and now I'm leaving without any panties under my dress. I feel like I'm in a fog. There could be a six-car pileup behind me, and I'd politely smile and nod and continue holding my hands on the wheel at two and ten. *Deep breaths in, deep breaths out.*

When my phone starts ringing beside me, I reach into my purse to retrieve it. I've been in such a state of shock since meeting him, I completely spaced on my promise to call Julie.

"Well? Did you meet him?" she asks.

"Yes, we just finished. I'm driving home."

"And? How was it? What was he like?"

"It was…interesting," I say, for lack of a better word.

"Is he a psycho?"

"No, he seemed completely normal. He's gorgeous, actually."

"So are you going to do it?"

"I don't know. It's crazy, right?" As I sit alone in my car, doubt starts to creep its way in.

"I think it's kinda cool. Going after what you want, putting yourself out there. You have lady balls, and I love that."

"I don't know about that." I realize it was smart of him to tell me to order a drink. Perhaps that's where my courage stemmed from.

My thoughts drift, and Julie's voice pulls me back into the moment.

"You should totally do it, Brie. You said he's gorgeous. Seriously, what's the problem? If you feel safe, I say why the hell not? Shit, maybe I'll sign up for a lesson with him myself if this works."

The idea of Julie touching him, of him growling out orders meant for her ears, isn't a pleasant one. It hits me like a smack to the face, and the insane urge to keep him all for myself flares up inside me. Shaking off the growing feelings as nothing more than casual interest tinged with lust, I maneuver my car into the underground garage of my building.

I park in my usual spot and grab my purse, exiting the car with the phone still pressed to my ear.

"I'm glad you're supportive of this," I tell her. "I thought you were going to think I was crazy." Actually, I considered not telling anyone what I was up to—even Julie—but then I realized that wasn't smart. He could turn out to be a serial killer. "I think this will be good for me."

I'm willing to put in the hard work to get what I want. Though, trust me, the idea of getting closer to Dom doesn't seem like work. He is intriguing and sexy in a domineering way. I've never been attracted to a man like him before, so I'm sure it was just a fluke. My boyfriends in college were certified geeks—glasses-wearing, white-tennis-shoe-sporting nerds from the IT lab. I almost giggle when I think about the differences between him and the men I'm used to. It's almost like comparing two opposing species. A lion to a guppy.

"I'm proud of you," Julie says. "When do you see him again? And you know I'm going to want more details, right?"

Heading inside the elevator, I laugh and punch the button for the sixth floor, where my apartment is located. "I'm well aware."

• • •

Lying in bed that night, I can't stop my mind from spinning, playing back my encounter with Dom. As I hug a pillow to my chest and burrow under the covers, I realize he took control prior to us even meeting, telling me how to dress, right down to my choice in underwear, and I eagerly obeyed. Maybe I have more of a submissive nature than I realized.

When I think about him inspecting the panties that he tucked into his pocket, a small smile uncurls on my lips. My life may be neat and well-ordered, but the panties that more closely resemble dental floss than underwear should signal to him that I'm open to a sexual adventure.

I feel naughty and slightly breathless, but if he can really help me win over Kirby, my decision is made. I'm going for it. Hell, it might even be fun.

Chapter Eight

HALE

Brielle followed through like a good little submissive.

By Thursday evening, waiting for me in my in-box is the signed nondisclosure agreement. It might not hold up in court, but it gives us both the peace of mind we need to pursue this affair discreetly. A second attachment contains her test results. She's completely clean. And her middle name is Gertrude. I suppress a chuckle.

I send her an e-mail, attaching my own recent test results. My name has been blacked out, but she'll learn that I'm twenty-eight and was born in Chicago. I tell her to meet me at a quiet, swanky lounge in downtown Chicago on Friday night. Our first lesson will begin then.

The Dominant in me is smirking at what I have in store for her.

• • •

I spot her immediately. Seated on a bar stool with a glass of white wine in front of her, Brielle is oblivious to the men's attention she's currently garnering. The plum-colored dress tied around her neck that dips low on her back, falling nearly to her ass, makes me feel oddly possessive. I clench my fists at my sides and take a deep breath.

"Who said you could wear a backless dress?" I whisper near her ear as I sidle up behind her. Brielle jumps as though my voice has startled her. She's not mine, she's only mine to train for the next six weeks, yet something about the men around her being treated to the graceful curve of her spine, the dimples in her lower back, bugs the fuck out of me.

Brielle looks stunning as she turns to face me with a worried expression. Her mouth forms into a pout, and her gaze travels the length of my body. Leaving late from work means I'm still dressed in a suit, though I've loosened the tie and unbuttoned my collar.

"I—" she begins.

"You look beautiful," I say, looking directly into her eyes.

"Thank you," she says softly, her posture relaxing.

I take the seat beside her and when the bartender approaches, I order a club soda.

Brielle watches me curiously. "You don't drink, do you?" she asks, her brow creasing.

"I never drink when I'm working, or when I'm playing in a scene. Keeping my head clear so I can focus on the woman I'm with is much more appealing than a cheap buzz."

She nods. "You're quite controlled, aren't you?"

"Most definitely."

"What do you do for fun?"

I smirk. "You want to know about my hobbies?"

"Why not?" She grins, bringing the glass of wine to her plump lips.

Something tells me that enlightening her about my activities at the club will only make her more nervous. And as fun as seeing that response would be, I need her to relax, open herself up, and trust me. Tonight will be our first time together. Still, she should know a little about the man she's hired.

"I like pushing women to their limits. Role playing, light bondage, spanking." I grin. "And on Sundays, I take my nana to church."

Brielle's mouth drops open.

"Tell me one thing about yourself that you wish you could change," I say, shifting the conversation to her.

She thinks for a moment before answering, taking another sip of her wine. "I wish I had more confidence. One of those women who can strut around in their birthday suit and feel like a goddess."

I don't know many women like that, but I know I can help her. It's as if a man has never really appreciated her body, shown her all the ways she's beautiful and amazing. I won't make the same mistake.

"And what about past relationships?" I ask. "You indicated you had two."

She nods. "Yes."

"How have you felt you were unsuccessful in those?"

"I was probably too eager, too ready for a steady relationship and monogamy, and the future that goes along with it," she admits. "Most men aren't interested in that."

She deserves monogamy and commitment from a man. But when have I ever really given that to a woman? Once, and it almost ended me.

"Tonight's lesson is centered on seduction. You wanted to practice attracting the opposite sex, flirting, yes?"

She nods, chewing on her lower lip.

"Do you see that man at the end of the bar?" The guy is in his mid-thirties, decent looking, and dressed in a suit and tie. No ring, nursing a bottle of beer in front of him. Basically, an easy target.

She nods.

"I want you to finish your wine. Walk over there, stand near him with your empty glass. Make eye contact, only briefly, then look away."

She swallows heavily, her cheeks brightening. The idea of this intimidates her, yet somehow I know she'll follow through. "Okay. And then what?"

I stroke her cheek, encouraging her bravery. "He'll start up a conversation with you. Be polite, but don't be too eager."

"Wait." She holds up her hand. "How do you know he'll start up a conversation with me?"

"He will. And he'll offer you another drink. Think it over, and then accept. Don't be too enthusiastic. You don't need him. You don't need a man at all, do you understand me?"

"But that's why I came to you. I want—"

I stop her mid-sentence. "Men can smell desperation a mile away. If he thinks you're aching for a ring on your finger and 2.5 kids, he'll disappear so fast your head will spin."

She frowns, and I suspect that my little overeager kitten has been going about things all wrong. Boldly making conversation, laughing at every bad joke, nodding along and agreeing to just about anything.

Fuck that. She is a delicacy to be savored. I want to breathe in her every breath, feel her skin warm beneath my hands, and know her moans of pleasure are because of me. And I want to fucking *work* for it. It's all in the chase. The submission is that much more beautiful when I have to work to make it happen.

"Talk with him for a few minutes, but let him take the lead. He's the man, for fuck's sake. I want you to practice flirting."

"I'm not good at flirting," she says.

My impish grins tells her *that's the entire point,* and when realization dawns, Brielle narrows her eyes.

"Your goal is to leave him wanting more. The old saying about giving away the milk for free? Let's just say it's entirely true. Leave him rock hard and breathless. Trust me, he'll be itching to call you."

She downs the remainder of her wine in a single gulp. "Wish me luck," she says, rising to her feet.

She's taller than I recall, and I look down to see her gracefully arched feet enhanced by black stilettos. "You won't need it," I mutter.

Brielle smirks and lets her long legs carry her over toward him, then does just as I've instructed. She stands beside him as if she's waiting for the bartender to notice her empty glass, and as I've predicted, Mr. Tall, Dark, and Douchey is already eyeing her up. He's practically fucking salivating.

He asks her to join him, motioning to the empty stool beside him. Brielle, my good little student, takes a moment to think it over rather than immediately agreeing.

She's a pleaser, and that's her problem. I want to teach her to stand on her own two feet, to realize her own worth, and make a man work for her affections.

No man wants a pushover. He wants the deep satisfaction that comes from conquering what hasn't been conquered before.

After a few minutes, she has a fresh drink in front of her, and she's smiling as she listens to something he says. She's attentive and interested, but only mildly so. He has to work for it, exactly as he should. I expect Brielle's eyes to dart occasionally over to mine, seeking approval, or just to check that I'm watching, but she doesn't look over even once. It bothers me more than it should.

Soon, she's leaning closer to him on the bar, openly laughing. As I watch them interact, I find myself wishing for something stronger than club soda. She's just a client, so my reaction is out of place. We hardly know each other yet.

Perhaps that's all it is—we've barely cemented our relationship, however brief it may be, and she's already off trying to please another man. That won't do. I haven't even gotten to sample the goods yet, and there's no way this douche is going to before me. We have an agreement. She's mine for six sessions.

Impatiently I watch them, waiting for an excuse to haul her ass out of here.

Her eyes are trained on him, and his hand is at her elbow. She removes her cell phone from her purse, and...the fuck? She's punching his number into her phone.

I rise and stride toward her, my vision blurred with the need to get her alone. My hand at her lower back surprises her, and she jumps slightly at my touch.

"Time to go, kitten," I bite out.

She swallows and gives a tight nod, allowing me to guide her from the stool. She doesn't say a word to the man beside her, but he watches us leave with his mouth hanging open.

I haul her toward the back hallway and stop once we're ensconced in shadows. Pressing her back to the wall, I pin her there with my hips.

"What the fuck was that?" I growl, well aware that I've just dragged her down the damn hallway like some caveman.

Blinking up at me with confusion, she gasps. "I was just doing what you asked!"

She's frustrated. Good. *Welcome to the club, sweetheart.*

I take her cell phone from her hand and stare down at it, letting the dissatisfaction I feel radiate from my features. "You took *his* number."

"And?"

I lean closer to her face, as close as I dare, so she can feel the wash of my warm breath and smell my scent. "Let the man be the man. He should take *your* number. *He* should call you first. *He* should plan the date."

Her gaze drops to the floor between us as she realizes her mistake.

I always have three scenarios in mind when going into a lesson. My goal is to push a client outside her comfort level, but depending on how she responds, I have other directions I can take things. Tonight, none of those scenarios accounted for me wanting to put her bare ass over my knee and redden her skin until her hot little cunt is wet, yet here we are. My hand is itching to smack her ass cheek. I take a deep breath, trying to regain the control I can feel slipping.

"You have one choice to make," I say, lifting her chin so she'll meet my eyes. "Decide now. A hotel, somewhere public, or your place."

The flash of understanding in her eyes tells me she knows this lesson isn't yet over; it's barely fucking begun. "My place," she says, surprising me.

I tug her toward the back entrance where my car is parked. My hand rests on her lower back as I guide her into the frosty air outside.

The need to get her alone and find out what turns her on, what makes her tremble, flares inside me. And the worried, timid look painted across her delicate features only makes me want her more.

Chapter Nine

BRIELLE

What am I doing?

I barely know this man, and yet I've punched my address into his fancy car's GPS. Now I'm practically trembling in the leather seat as we drive toward my apartment. Other than asking for my address, he hasn't said a word, and his silence is unnerving.

I grab my phone and send a text to Julie.

BRIELLE: Shit! I invited him back to my place. Talk me out of this!!

Her reply is instant.

JULIE: Go for it, girl!

Not the words of caution I wanted to hear. Then again, she's always encouraged me to take more risks, so what was I really expecting? I take a deep breath and catch Dom looking at me from the corner of his eye.

"Everything okay over there?" he asks, pulling me from my moment of panic.

"I…yes."

"Don't lie to me, Brielle. You're second-guessing yourself."

I drop my hands into my lap and stare straight ahead. "Why ask if you already knew that?"

"Tell me why," he says, his voice firm and commanding.

"It's not every day I invite a strange man over to my house."

"I sure as fuck hope not. But you've texted your friend that you're bringing me home, which is exactly what you should do. Just relax, okay?"

It's unsettling how he can read me so well. Not to mention, his abrupt change in mood is unexpected. I can't possibly begin to imagine what's going on inside his head.

"But I thought you were mad at me about earlier...I thought you were going to spank me," I admit softly.

"Do you want me to spank you?"

My gaze cuts to his large palms curled around the steering wheel, and a warm shiver of anticipation pulses through me.

"No," I say, but my denial sounds weak and hollow, even to my ears.

His mouth lifts in a lazy smile.

When we reach my apartment, he parallel parks on the street. I lead him inside, fumbling with my keys as I unlock the front door to the building. Inside the elevator, I hit the button for the sixth floor and glance over at him. He's pinned me with one of those intense, icy stares that I can feel deep inside my body.

"This male friend of yours, Kirby…have you two ever shared a drunken hookup?" he asks, completely surprising me.

"No."

"A kiss?" he asks, stalking closer.

"Does it matter?" I've never done anything remotely sexual with Kirby, but his insistence at knowing these details seems too intimate, since I know nothing of his past.

He makes a low sound in his throat, closes the distance between us, and dips his head to inhale the scent of my neck. "When I ask a question, I expect an honest answer."

He lingers at my neck, and the heat from his breath warms my skin. For a moment, I worry my heavy breathing will give me away. His dominating side is sexy as sin, and I want to see more of it.

"Never, okay?" I whisper. My feelings and reactions to him confuse me.

The elevator stops, and I lead him to my apartment.

The moment the door closes behind us, I reach for the light switch, but his hand catches my wrist. Somehow I'm pinned against the wall, his large form holding me in place with my wrists locked above my head. My heart jumps into my throat as I wonder what will happen next. Raw sexual chemistry burns hotly between us; there's no denying the attraction. And I have a feeling things are about to get real.

"I'm going to kiss you. This is your chance to say yes or no." His grip is firm, yet his voice is soft.

Indecision rips through me. I should say no; we're working together. This isn't about romance and flowers. But I want his lips on mine more than I want my next breath.

"Yes."

The second the word leaves my lips, his mouth is on mine, dominating me with a rush of hungry kisses. His lips move against mine while his hand adjusts my jaw to just the right angle, and when he finds it, his tongue sweeps out and licks at mine.

Damn, the man can kiss. A weakness sweeps over me and my knees nearly give out.

When he releases my hands, I claw at his suit jacket, wanting him closer. His huge, heavy erection presses against my belly, and my inner muscles clench in delicious anticipation.

His hands slide down my body until they find my ass. He grips my butt, one cheek in each rough palm, kneading and squeezing as he groans into my mouth. My panties dampen instantly.

When he pulls his mouth from mine, I gasp for breath, feeling disoriented like I've just run a marathon. And fuck, that was from just one kiss.

"Were you going to let that man touch your wet little pussy?" His voice is deep and slightly breathless.

"No!" I gasp.

"That's right you're not. He did nothing to earn that privilege. And for the next six weeks, this pussy is mine. Say it, Brielle."

"For the next six weeks, I'm yours."

"Not good enough. Say it."

"My pussy is yours." My intimate muscles clench as the words leave my mouth.

"That's right," he says, moving his hand over the front of my dress to cup my sex through the fabric. "Mine." When my hips involuntarily push toward his hand, he meets my eyes with a serious expression. "It's been too long, hasn't it, peach? Should I let you come so you're able to focus on our lesson?"

I make a weak, desperate sound in my throat, my lust-fogged brain fighting with myself to hold it together when...*oh.*

His hands slip beneath the hem of my dress and tug my panties down my hips. The black thong slips to my ankles, stopping at my heels. I must be quite a sight, pinned against the wall with my underwear at my feet.

He pets the seam of my sex, parting me, and when he finds me slick, he glides his fingers through my folds and groans. Then he brings his fingers to his mouth and tastes them. My cheeks become warm and

I'm overcome with a strange feeling. Reverence? Desire?

"Fuck, you taste good."

After licking his fingers clean, he lowers his hand again and plunges two fingers deep inside me, causing me to cry out from the sudden and very pleasurable invasion.

"Have to get this ready for me. I don't want to hurt you," he growls, thrusting two fingers in and out.

I latch onto his biceps, hanging on for dear life. Pleasure explodes inside me, and nothing has ever felt quite so good. My head thumps back against the wall when his thumb rubs between my thighs. His fingers slide deep inside me, stroking, pleasing me as no man has before.

When his mouth lowers to mine again and he bites my bottom lip, I explode, coming so intensely, I see a burst of white light behind my eyelids. I gasp for air, my eyes opening to find his.

"Do you always come so fast, peach?" he asks.

I don't answer. I simply stand there, hanging on to him as I fight to catch my breath.

"You're beautiful when you let go."

He releases his hold on me and brings one hand to my cheek, where he uses the pad of his thumb to carefully stroke my lower lip. Reminded of how he bit me, I flinch, but he kisses away the sting, murmuring an apology. It's dizzying how he can be so domineering and rough one moment, and then sweet and tender the next.

He leans in close, as calm and collected as ever. "Go into your bedroom, take off your dress, kneel on the floor, and wait for me."

Despite my intense release mere moments ago, my body is hungry for more. More of everything. Those skillful kisses, rough hands, and the filthy words meant to make me submit.

I reach down to pull my panties back up, when a firm hand on my wrist stops me.

He shakes his head. "Who said you could put those back on?" He helps me step out of my panties and dangles them from his index finger. "My sexy little peach," he murmurs.

When he tucks my discarded panties into his pocket, I know I've been dismissed.

My shaky legs carry me down the short, dark hallway into my bedroom. I'm unsure if I should turn on the light, but decide to do exactly as he asked. With trembling fingers, I untie the strings at the back of my neck and let the dress pool at my feet, then step out of my heels and place everything beside my dresser.

Once I'm completely nude, I kneel in the center of the room with my gaze trained on the floor and wait. My heartbeat is crashing against my ribs, and I'm filled with a strange sense of longing and anticipation. Sex is never like this. It's always been in a bed, under the covers, without any dirty talk or forceful commands. Simple and straightforward. I know sex with my Dom is going to be anything but ordinary. And that's way more exciting than it should be.

As I kneel in my darkened bedroom, naked and wet between my legs, the noise in my brain begins to quiet. I'm singularly focused on him. My gaze never strays from its focus on the floor near the door, on the swath of light that comes from the hall. My heartbeat grows heavy with anticipation.

Minutes pass and I hear a door close. Did he leave?

I fight with myself, wanting to stand up and go to the window and see if he's left, but my body demands I stay put. So I continue waiting in my spot and several minutes later, I hear him. Footsteps coming closer.

When he enters the room, he's carrying some type of small black leather bag. My heart riots in my chest.

He calmly crosses the room, all but ignoring me, and sets the bag on my bed. I don't know if I should watch, but I can't help my eyes from following him. He removes his suit jacket and neatly folds it, placing it on the table beside my bed. He unzips the bag and removes a black strip of fabric, and then turns to face me.

"Those greedy little eyes want to see everything, to form an opinion on it all, yes?"

I don't answer. My breathing grows shallow as I continue watching him.

"The only thing I want you focused on is sensation, feeling. Do you understand?"

"Yes."

"I want to show you what you're capable of. Do you trust me?"

"Yes," I say again. I'm not sure why, but I do. And trust me, I'm aware it's absolutely insane.

He stands behind me and fastens the silk fabric over my eyes, tying it behind my head. It blocks my vision entirely. My heart rate increases as the realization that I'm in total darkness sinks in.

I listen closely and hear him walk toward the bed. Then I hear a match spark to life, and my entire body stiffens. His footsteps cross the room, and I'm about to ask what's going on when the faint scent of sandalwood and black currant greets me. He's lit a candle, I'm pretty sure. Maybe this is all part of a ritual for him. Nothing is rushed, everything is calculated and planned out, and I like that he's taken so much time and care into planning my lessons.

I hear one loud thud and then another. He's removed his shoes, I think.

"Hands behind your back." He's directly in front of me now. I can feel the heat emanating from his body.

I do as he's asked and lace my fingers together at the small of my back. The new position pushes my breasts forward and out. I imagine what I must look like naked, blindfolded, and kneeling on the floor, bathed in the soft flicker of candlelight. *Well, this is new.*

"Such a pretty sight, peach."

As he strokes my cheek with his thumb, I lean in toward his touch, feeling approval in every stroke of his fingertips. His hands continue their soft caresses, trailing down my neck and through the long tresses of my hair. His touch is gentle, restrained, as if he's holding himself back. For now, at least.

"We need to discuss your limits. Are there things you're uncomfortable with, Brielle?"

I'm not sure how to answer, because while there are things that make me nervous, a small voice inside me says that's the entire point. I want to grow in confidence and in experience, and the only way to grow is to push myself outside my comfort zone.

I recall the quote taped to my fridge: *Life begins at the end of your comfort zone.*

When he trails his hand down my lower back, I realize I haven't responded yet. My ass is exposed in this position and he takes full advantage, brushing the pad of his thumb over my backside and stroking me there.

"Is this fair game?" he asks, his voice rough.

His warm finger in a forbidden place causes little fractures of heat to radiate down my spine, and butterflies take flight in my belly. Since I couldn't form words right now if I wanted to, I merely nod.

"Hmm. Naughty thing," he says under his breath. He pulls his hand away and lifts my chin, even though eye contact is impossible with the blindfold. But perhaps there's something he needs to see in my expression, in my reactions to him.

"You need to choose a safe word. Something easy to remember. If I do something you don't like, use it and I'll stop. Understand?"

"Yes," I whisper, the need growing inside me.

"So, what'll it be?"

"I-I'm not sure. Any suggestions?" I ask.

"It needs to be something easy to remember when you're getting your ass handed to you—literally." I can hear the playful smirk in his voice.

The word is on my lips before I have time to process it. "Peach."

"Perfect," he says adoringly.

I hear a zipper being tugged down slowly. A faint trace of soap tickles my nose, along with masculine musk. All of my senses are finely tuned in to what's happening just beyond my reach.

"I'm going to show you how to pleasure a man with your mouth, Brielle. Would you like that?"

The sound of skin rubbing together sends my mind spinning—I imagine he's freed his cock and his hand is sliding up and down. His breathing grows harsh, and I can feel myself getting wet.

I told him at our first meeting that performing oral sex makes me uncomfortable, which is probably why he's making that our first lesson. "Y-yes, please." I don't know who this woman on the floor begging to suck his cock is, but there's complete honesty in my reactions to him. It seems his dominant nature brings out a side of me I didn't know existed until this very moment.

"Open for me," he says.

I open my mouth wide and wait.

"Wider, sweetheart." I can hear a hint of dark humor in his voice.

I force my mouth even wider and feel the blunt head of him caress my lips. My tongue darts out instinctively to taste what he's offering. A grunt pushes past his lips as my tongue swirls around the head of him.

Then he eases forward and fills my mouth. Every sense is heightened with my vision obstructed, and I soak up every detail I can. The vein that runs along the side of his length. The slightly salty taste at the tip of him, the heavy weight of his balls when my tongue ventures lower.

"Take it, sweetheart. Take me deep."

I swallow him down, my throat closing around his massive girth, and he grunts. Pride surges through me.

Each time he glides over my lower lip, I'm reminded of where he bit me earlier. It's swollen and sore, but in the best way possible.

"That's it," he says to encourage me, his voice impossibly tight. "A man wants to feel how into it you are. He wants to know you're enjoying yourself too."

I am into it, more than I've ever been. I think the difference is this dominant man and my need to please him. Unlacing my fingers, I grip his impressive length, stroking as I suck him.

His hands slide through my hair, and he gives a firm tug. The sting of pain is slight and dissipates quickly. "Hands behind your back."

I pull back and instinctively lift my chin to gaze up at him, even though I can't see him. "I want to touch you."

"You are touching me. Your mouth feels incredible, pet."

I soar at his compliment and place my hands behind me again so I can resume where I left off, my open mouth seeking him in the darkness. His hands on either side of my face guide me forward and his hips begin rocking, pushing his thick cock in and out of my mouth. I am a vessel for his pleasure, and nothing could please me more.

As the intoxicating scent of the burning candle fills the room, I'm consumed by him and by all the sensations. This big man looming over me, my mouth open so wide my jaw aches, and my pussy so wet and greedy, it clenches each time he thrusts forward.

"Stop." His voice is raw, and he pulls his cock from my mouth with a wet sucking sound. Growling out a curse, he leaves me to wonder what I've done wrong. "You lied to me, Brielle."

He strips off my blindfold and the flicker of candlelight greets me, illuminating the fact that I'm on my knees with him standing over me. His cock stands tall, glistening with my saliva. His body is smooth everywhere, sculpted of rock-hard muscle. This man is built for sex.

"What did I do?" I ask as my brain struggles to comprehend what I've lied to him about.

Shit. *What have I done?*

He grips his cock and squeezes, staring down at me with displeasure. "You led me to believe you weren't good at sucking cock. And you're going to make me come if you keep that up."

Pride swells inside me, and I suck my lip into my mouth in an effort to fight off a smile.

"You want to finish me? To feel me lose control in your mouth?" He tilts his head and studies me.

"Yes," I say confidently, staring straight up at him.

"Bend over. Place your forehead on the carpeting and put that pretty little ass in the air."

I do as he's instructed, my body already tingling in anticipation of what's to come. I am completely exposed, and while normally I'd feel embarrassed and unsure with him, I feel alive.

"Ease your knees apart."

When I spread my knees apart, I'm completely open for his perusal. I should feel self-conscious, but with my cheek pressed to the floor, I look up and see the longing in his eyes. A hot bolt darts through me. I feel more desirable in this moment than I ever recall feeling before.

"And to think I was going to take it slow with you, ease you into things tonight." He makes a low tsk-tsking sound under his breath.

Am I being punished? Why does that excite me so much?

"This ass needs to be fucked," he murmurs, gripping one fleshy cheek before treating it to a sharp swat.

I release a grunt at the unexpected contact.

"Be still. And stay quiet," he says, his voice devoid of all fun and games.

I wait, my behind on prominent display as I wonder what will happen next.

When he drops to his knees behind me and presses his face between my cheeks, I jump and shout out a little yelp.

He grips my hips. "Quiet. And be still," he reminds me.

I swallow and ease back into position, feeling his mouth at my core once again. The warmth of his tongue as it sweeps over me, the sharp nip of his teeth raking across my swollen clit—it feels incredible, and his skill at this is enough to make me forget my name. But he doesn't focus anywhere for long, he licks and caresses me with his tongue, but every time I'm close to the edge, he changes his angle and pressure so I'm left reeling and unsatisfied.

"Please," I beg, needing a release.

He plunges two fingers deep inside me and focuses all his attention on my oversensitive clit, sending me hurtling toward orgasm in a dizzying rush of excitement.

"Yes, yes," I beg, right on the edge.

His hand smacks my ass again, a reminder to be quiet for him, but thank God, he doesn't stop that wicked mouth from devouring me.

My orgasm crashes into me, pulling a low moan from my throat, and my fingers dig into the carpeting, scrambling for purchase.

"That's it, peach," he murmurs encouragingly against my backside as he slowly removes his fingers.

My entire world is rocked. I feel spent and used in the most lovely way.

"Up on your knees, pet."

I couldn't rise to my feet right now if he demanded it. But he helps me up to my knees and as soon as I'm perched before him again, I open wide, waiting for him to take my mouth again. The admiration in his gaze makes my belly flip. Without direction, he pushes forward, shoving his huge cock into my throat, and he holds my head in place, fucking my mouth as he desires.

I gag slightly and he retreats; his eyes trained on mine flash with something dark. "Don't stop now," he warns.

I shake my head; I won't stop until he makes me. I want to use my hands, and he hasn't expressly forbid it this time, so with this cock bobbing in and out of my mouth, I test the waters, trailing my fingernails over his solid thighs. When he doesn't stop me, I grow bold, wrapping both fists firmly around his generous length and stroking him between each thrust.

"Fuck." The word rumbles from deep in his chest, an almost animalistic sound. Seconds later, his fists tighten in my hair and a hot jet of semen coats my throat.

I swallow him down and once he's finished, he bends forward and brushes his lips over my forehead, then pulls on black boxer briefs.

My limbs are heavy, and all the blood has settled into my lower half from remaining on my knees for so long. I'm shivering and weak.

"Come here," he says, gathering me up in his arms and moving me onto the bed. He pulls the quilt over me and holds me quietly. After several minutes, he tilts my chin up as though he's inspecting me. His eyes are dark and stormy, and I don't understand why. "Are you okay?"

"Yes." My voice comes out hoarse and rough.

"Would you like some water?" he asks.

I nod.

"I'll be right back. Just lie back and rest."

He rises from the bed, and I watch his tight butt as he heads for my kitchen. In the silence, my gaze wanders to the candle he's placed on my dresser, its flame dancing in the otherwise dark room.

The initial satisfaction fades and a deep shame over what I've done—with a perfect stranger, a man I've hired—threatens to overwhelm me. Confused by the quick shift in my emotions, I blink back tears.

I rest my eyes for a few moments and when I open them, he's standing over me wearing nothing more than boxers that barely contain him and the generous swell at the front. His eyes are soulful, and his look is one of concern. He brings a glass of cool water to my lips, and I take a long drink, grateful for his compassion.

"Are you okay with everything that happened?" he asks, noticing my solemn mood.

"Yes, I'm fine." It was just a blow job, for goodness' sake. But I think some part of me knows it's only the tip of the iceberg. Submission. Blindfolds. What's next? Before I have time to ponder that, his cell phone rings.

He apologizes as he grabs his pants from the floor and fishes his phone from the pocket. As he looks down at the screen, he frowns. "Do you mind if I answer? It might be something important."

"It's fine."

When he hits a button, the sound of feminine voice crying in the otherwise silent room startles us both. In the darkened room, he must have inadvertently activated the speaker phone.

"Hale?" she sobs, her voice frantic.

He quickly takes the phone off speaker and presses it to his ear. "Yeah, it's me. I'm here." His tone is soothing, worried.

Hale...is that his name? What kind of name is that? It's surprisingly fitting. Its association with the weather, forceful and a little scary, is just like him. I love it. I wonder who the woman is, a sister? A friend? My stomach sinks when I realize she could be another client.

It's impossible not to listen, and he makes no move to leave the room or prevent me from overhearing. Whoever the woman is, she's sobbing, and though I can't make out what she's saying, he listens attentively, repeatedly telling her that everything will be okay in a solemn and comforting tone. After several minutes of kind encouragements, he tells her that he's not alone, and that he has to go. He ends the conversation by telling her to run a warm bath and make herself a mug of tea, and that he will check on her later.

When he hangs up, his posture is so rigid he looks like he could crush the phone in his hand. He releases a heavy sigh. "I'm sorry about that."

Of course I want to ask who the mystery woman is, but remember we've made an agreement not to delve into each other's personal lives. "Is...is she okay?"

"Do you know what aftercare is, Brielle?"

"No."

"Chrissy is a submissive at a club I belong to. She was shaken up after a rough scene with a Dom tonight, and he left before she could talk with him about what she had just experienced."

"And she trusted you to talk her through it?"

"Yes." He places his hand against mine and meets my eyes. "We will always talk about how you're feeling after a lesson. I won't leave until I know you're okay. And if you have questions, or unexpected emotions pop up afterward, you can call me. I have a cell phone number for clients that I'll give you."

"Okay."

"I'm sorry tonight's lesson got cut short. I didn't intend for that to happen."

"That's okay. It sounds like she needed you."

I wonder what that means, a submissive at a club he belongs to. A sex club? Does he play with her too? A pang of jealousy flares inside me, but I ignore it. He's a Dominant hired by scores of women for sexual instruction, yet there's no denying he's a caring partner. I'm not mad; I'm more curious than anything.

"How many women are you mentoring?"

His hand comes to rest on my shoulder. "You're the only one I'm concerned with."

His non-answer sets me at ease more than it should. "So, what does aftercare usually involve?"

He hands me my glass of water, encouraging me to drink more. "It can be discussion over what just happened, cuddling, kissing, or even vanilla intercourse if the scene didn't involve sex." He waits while I consider everything I've learned tonight, and tucks the quilt tighter around me. "Any other questions?"

I meet his eyes and smile. "Now that I know your name...can I call you Hale?"

He chuckles and nods his head. "You may."

Chapter Ten

HALE

I'm waiting for Reece to arrive at the bistro we agreed on for lunch, but all my thoughts are on Brielle and the night we shared.

Kirby must be a fucking idiot. If he hasn't noticed her by now, that's his problem. I know I'll walk away at the end of this, like I always do, but I'll enjoy every single one of my sessions with Brielle in the meantime.

I pull out my phone, deciding to text her. We exchanged numbers before I left last night.

HALE: How are you feeling today?

BRIELLE: Good.

HALE: Not sore are you?

BRIELLE: A little.

HALE: I'm having lunch with an old friend, but I wanted to check on you. I apologize our lesson got cut short. I promise you that's not a regular occurrence.

BRIELLE: It's okay. Learning your name was worth it. ;)

I chuckle to myself, liking her sassy side.

HALE: One more thing, pet. I'm not free until Friday this week. You are not allowed to masturbate. I'm the only one touching that sweet pussy. Is that clear?

BRIELLE: Yes, sir.

Her use of the word *sir* is unexpected and quite welcome. Initially, she questioned herself, me, and this whole process. But it turns out that with only the slightest coaching, she is submitting beautifully.

"How's your newest project?" Reece asks as he strolls toward me.

"She's a natural," I remark, lifting my gaze from my phone. I won't be one of those douche bags glued to his phone, no matter how entertaining I find my newest pet project.

Pulling out a chair, Reece sits down across from me. "A natural submissive, huh?" He makes a deep, appreciative noise in his throat.

Damn straight. My little peach is a pleaser. It's up to me to show her how to funnel her energy. She doesn't need to throw herself at every man who gives her a passing glance; she only needs to submit to her Dom when he demands it. It makes my cock ache just thinking about it.

I've found myself thinking of her all day long. Usually that's the case when I'm working with a client, but it's most often that I'm analyzing my own performance, thinking of ways to improve my teaching. But aside from my fuckup with leaving my phone on, I haven't thought of my lesson once. I've thought of Brielle's sweet ass in the air, her pink pussy slick and wet from my words alone, and the breathless whimper she makes when she comes.

"What are you smiling at, brother?" Reece asks, giving me a grin.

"Just the woman I'm coaching. She's...fun." I smile back.

"Fun." He chuckles, his eyes on mine. "You gonna keep this one?"

Given my past, he knows how raw his words make me feel. "No," I choke out. "I'm training her for another man."

He nods. "I see." He picks up the menu and glances at it, but I can see his wheels turning. "You're not going to have a hard time giving her up, are you?"

"God, no." I shudder. After what happened the last time, that's not a possibility for me. Reece knows that as well as I do.

We place our order with the young waitress that Reece can barely keep his eyes off of, and make small talk about work.

"How's Chrissy?" I ask in between bites of my sirloin sandwich. "She called me last night, distraught. Needed to be talked down off the ledge. Sounds like she worked with someone new who didn't know what the fuck he was doing."

Reece would call me a pussy, but aftercare has always been one of my favorite parts. Talking about what we just experienced together, laying it all out there in the open. Examining it and letting all of the feelings of lust, pain, and desire refuse to hide in the shadows. Submission is a beautiful thing, and I'm always glad to explore it in words after the act itself. To make sure my partner felt as good about it as I did. Plus, I'm serious about this mentor thing. I damn well want to know if something I did caused real pain, physical or emotional, and I want to learn, to grow. A Dominant is only as strong as the communication he receives from his partner.

He adjusts his water glass, looking uncomfortable. "Yeah, we had some fucking jackass fly in from New York City for the weekend. Called himself Dominic." He scoffs. "Turns out he was nothing more than an amateur. But you know Chrissy. She was eager for release, putting herself front and center, ready to be used however he wanted."

Fucking Chrissy. I inhale deeply, frustration creeping its way into my posture. I flex my hands, my knuckles popping with the effort.

Reece holds up a palm. "I know, brother. I'm pissed off about it too. Trust me, I won't make that mistake again. That fucker and the guy who vouched for him are both banned for life."

"Good." The one-word, grunted response is all I'm capable of.

That unpleasantness out of the way, we focus on our food as we catch up on small talk like men often do. Sports, politics, and women. I keep waiting for Reece to announce he's collared a sub, that he's finally found his match, but so far it hasn't happened.

He seems content to dabble in the lifestyle, but deep down, I know he's seeking something more.

During lunch, I find myself smiling, thinking about Brielle and planning our next lesson. Balancing my work and social calendar with my mentoring is often difficult, but I've always preferred it that way. Staying busy keeps my mind from wandering, which has always been a good thing.

So why am I hesitant to get involved with another client right now? I have two other women I've just wrapped up with, but last night while scanning the e-mails in my gentleman mentor in-box, I was unsure if I wanted to get involved with anyone else right now.

I tell myself it's not due to Brielle, but part of me knows it is.

Chapter Eleven

BRIELLE

"Push your bottom back and press your heels into the floor."

I glance up at the yoga instructor and mimic her pose, pushing back into a downward-facing-dog position.

Frustrated, I glance at Julie beside me. She's so tall and graceful with her long limbs and perfect posture; her downward dog looks nothing like my awkward, shaking attempt. Yet week after week, I let her drag me here to this yoga studio and twist my body into shapes it isn't meant to do, following it up with a wheat-grass shot that I can barely stomach, all in the name of good health. *Oh, joy.*

I glance at the clock and see that it's only been seven minutes. *Shit*. I'm doomed.

"I still need the details about the other night," Julie hisses at me.

"And yet you bring me to yoga, which I hate." I narrow my eyes. I'd be much more inclined to give her all the juicy details over, say, margaritas.

"It's a free country, Brie. You didn't have to come. I think you secretly like it." She winks.

I shoot her a scowl and blow a lock of hair from my face.

"Besides, I think that Dom of yours will appreciate how limber you are," she adds.

"He's not mine," I tell her. Apparently, I'm one of many.

His phone call last night with Chrissy springs to mind again. The soft, calming tone of his voice, the anguish in his features as he spoke to her. It was like catching a glimpse of a whole different side to him, one that I never imagined existed.

"And rise up into warrior pose. Arms gracefully extend out from your body," the instructor says from the front of the room. "Brielle, lengthen your spine, chin up. Good."

I roll my eyes and inhale deeply. My brain is still spinning over my arrangement with Hale. I hope I'm doing the right thing.

This is all for Kirby, I remind myself. I can do this.

• • •

When Friday rolls around, I'm distracted and edgy. I didn't hear from Hale all week, aside from his text this morning.

HALE: Are you ready for your lesson tonight?

BRIELLE: Of course. Are we meeting for a drink again?

HALE: No. Not this time. When I fuck you, I want you stone-cold sober and one hundred percent sure this is what you want.

Needless to say, I found myself speechless and still haven't responded. After my second cup of coffee, I finally summon the courage.

BRIELLE: Do you want to meet at my place?

HALE: Yes. I'll be there at 7 p.m. Make sure you eat something beforehand. You'll need your energy.

When darkness falls, I finally force myself to leave the office. It's Friday, which means all of my coworkers took off early, looking forward to their weekends and asking me if I had any plans. I mumbled something noncommittal about seeing a friend.

If they knew the truth, my professional reputation would be at stake, and I can't have that. I may still be new to my career, but I'm a damn good real estate agent, and I won't risk it.

I gather up my laptop bag, my purse, and the remnants of the lunch I was too nervous to eat, then head out to the parking lot. I knew staying at the office and keeping myself busy with listings and e-mails would be a better decision than pacing my quiet apartment, waiting for Hale. The anticipation of seeing him makes my belly flip. I have no idea what he has in store for me tonight, aside from his hint that we'd be fucking.

Once home, I only have an hour until Hale's due to arrive. I secure my hair into a bun, strip down, and wash off in the shower. Then I stand naked in front of my dresser, peering down into my underwear drawer. Both times we met up, I've worn sexy G-strings, and both times he's kept my panties as some type of intimate souvenir.

My eyes flash on my most nondescript pair of white cotton briefs. *I wonder what he'll say if I wear those?*

A streak of defiance flares within me and an impish grin curls my mouth. Wanting to force a reaction from him, I grab the panties and step into them, then add a plain white bra, a pair of jeans, and a comfy long-sleeved pink tee. We're staying in, after all. What's the point in dressing up?

Once I'm ready, I munch on a handful of pretzels as I tidy up my apartment. I know Hale told me to eat, but the idea of sitting down to a full, heavy meal is not appealing. A glass of wine sounds fantastic right about now, but I won't indulge. Hale wants me completely sober, and there's something ironically intoxicating about that.

The buzz of the intercom catches me off guard.

He's here.

I press the button and tell him to come on up. Moments later, feeling breathless and excited, I answer the door and find the tall, striking man I'm coming to know as my Dom standing in the hall. He's dressed down tonight in dark-washed jeans and a slim-cut Henley in navy blue.

"No suit and tie tonight," I murmur.

"No. I left the office early and went home, so I had time to change."

"Oh." Never having seen him in anything other than a suit, I stand mutely in my doorway, struck by how his straight-fit jeans hug him in all the right places, and how the shirt brings out how intensely blue his eyes are.

"May I come in, peach?" he asks with an amused expression as if he knows I've been standing here awestruck by him.

"Of course." I pull the door wider and usher him inside.

It's his second time here, but I didn't give him much of a tour the first time. He pretty much attacked me at the front door and carried me to my room after our sexually-charged encounter in the bar. Tonight's mood feels mellow in contrast. Something tells me we're going to take our time, explore things more fully this time around. I'm both nervous and excited.

I lead him from the entryway, stopping at the kitchen to ask, "Would you like something to drink?"

"I'm fine. Thank you."

Heading to the living room, I watch his gaze bounce around the room as if he's not only taking in my space, but deciphering my personality too. He wanders over to the bookshelves lining the far wall. They are crammed with paperbacks of every variety and genre.

"Bookworm, huh?" He lifts my signed copy of the mega-bestselling erotic romance from its revered resting place.

"I read on my iPad, but I buy my favorites in paperback too," I explain.

"Romance, mystery, paranormal." He skims his fingers along their spines. "You like it all, don't you?" I can't help but catch the flirty tone to his comment.

"Yes, but love stories are my favorite."

"Why's that?" He turns to face me, his expression turning serious.

"Because. It's what everyone wants, isn't it? A partner. Someone to comfort you at the end of a hard day. Someone to love."

He frowns at me. "Not everyone wants that."

I want to challenge him, to prove him wrong. I don't even know why, other than that my belief in love is everything to me, and I will fight to defend it.

"What do you want then?" I lift my chin, trying to force a response from him.

His narrowed eyes latch onto mine. "I'm in charge. Don't forget that. If I were looking for love, don't you think I'd have a girlfriend? A wife?"

"Of course," I stammer, getting the distinct feeling I've somehow offended him. "You're attractive, intelligent. I didn't mean to suggest—"

"What I want is you on all fours, tits down, ass up." His eyes darken, and I can feel the challenge radiating off of him.

I'm unnerved and thrown off-balance. His reaction to my declaration that surely everyone must be looking for love was met with harsh rejection that only someone who's been hurt would have. The unmistakable feeling that he's been heartbroken washes over me. Is that why he does all this? This control? This no-strings mentoring?

Before I can ponder it further, his hands on my shoulders bring me back to the moment. With steady pressure, he guides me down to my knees, all but signaling our discussion is over.

Gazing up at him, I sink to the carpeting. I hate that he's shut down our conversation, but recalling our previous lesson, I remember the intense look in his eyes, the almost primal need that seemed to take over. Afterward, he was tender and sweet, and seemed much more willing to engage in pillow talk. So I decide to be a good little submissive during my lesson, and then once he's satisfied and feeling content, try to get some information out of him. I'm beyond curious about this man I've agreed to work with.

"Did you follow my instruction this week, Brielle?" he asks.

My gaze flits around the room as my brain struggles to remember what I was supposed to do this week.

"You didn't touch yourself, did you?" he asks.

Oh. "No, sir."

He walks around me so that he's positioned directly in front of me. My eyes are level with his groin, and I can't help the smile that tugs on my lips.

"What is it, pet?" he asks, lightly stroking my cheek.

"Nothing." I cough to cover up my smile.

"Tell me." His tone is firm, and I know there's no way I'm going to disobey, despite the truth being quite embarrassing.

"I was just remembering when I...sucked you."

He lifts his chin, looking up at the ceiling briefly, before bringing his gaze back down to mine. "You enjoyed that, didn't you?"

"Yes." My cheeks flush, but it's the unabashed truth.

His fingertips stroke my throat, running along the column of my neck, and every vivid detail about having his thick length in my mouth rushes back. The bite of discomfort in my jaw, drawing shaky breaths in through my nose, his pungent scent, the groans of pleasure that rumbled in his chest. I'm growing wet already.

"If you behave tonight, I might let you suck on my cock again. But first, tonight's lesson, yes?" he asks.

I nod, eager to learn all he has to offer.

"Tonight is about you understanding your sex appeal. Practicing the art of lovemaking, without any self-consciousness. Appreciating the true effect you have on a man, Brie."

I swallow my nerves. "Do I affect you?" I whisper, gazing up at him.

"Does this answer your question?" His hand leaves my cheek, and he grips the bulge at the front of his trousers. *Dear God.* "You've got me hard already, sweetheart. At nothing more than the thought of getting to fuck your tight little pussy tonight. You are a prize, and I'm lucky to have you. Any man would be lucky to have you. Say it for me."

"Any man would be lucky to have me," I murmur.

His hand strokes my hair. "We're going to work on getting you to actually believe that, but good, for now." Offering me his hand, he helps me rise to my feet. His mood seems to have softened, and I'm still trying to catch up. Treating me to a warm and unexpected kiss on the mouth, Hale leans in to whisper near my ear. "Go into your bedroom. Undress and wait for me on the bed. I want to see what kind of sexy panties you've chosen for me tonight."

I walk to my darkened bedroom and undress, only remembering my plain white briefs when I remove my jeans. I remove everything but the panties and lie back on the bed.

Soon, Hale is back, carrying his black bag.

The nerves in my belly do a little dance in anticipation of what he has inside that mysterious bag of his.

Setting the bag down, he removes his candle and lights it, placing it on my dresser.

Familiar notes of sandalwood and black currant warm the room, and my nerves dissipate slightly. I have a feeling that I'll forever associate this scent with him, and I don't quite know how I feel about that.

I'm not sure if I'm allowed to ask him questions at this juncture, but my curiosity gets the best of me. "What's with the candle, anyway? Not that I don't love the scent, I'm just curious."

"It's another way for me to set the scene. A Dominant needs to be in control at all times, in all things. It's a scent I had custom made for me. It provides another way for me to ensure the submissive I'm training is using all five senses in a way she hasn't before during lovemaking."

"I see."

I wait to see what accoutrement or device he'll withdraw from the bag next, but he turns to face me, letting his eyes wander the length of me.

"Sorry, they're not sexy," I apologize, looking down at my choice in underwear.

His smirk tells me he's about to prove me wrong. "Are you sure about that, peach?" Sitting down beside me, he runs his thumb along the seam of the panties, tracing where the hem meets my inner thigh.

I'm eager to feel his touch between my thighs, though I'm quite enjoying the reverent look in his eyes as he studies me. My gaze follows his path as his thumb moves to the front of my panties where my plump outer lips feel sensitive and swollen. He rubs up and down, making my clit tingle with each swipe of his finger.

I can feel myself getting wet, and I know he must feel the way the damp fabric clings to me.

"I want to fuck you with these on," he growls, proving every notion I've had about myself to be wrong. He finds me desirable, even in my most modest state, and the thought thrills me.

"Anything you want."

He raises one eyebrow. "Are you sure about that?"

The memory of him telling me he wanted to take me, well, *there*, is still fresh in my mind. "I'm sure," I say, mustering my courage. *Be brave.* This is my time for adventure, to explore.

Leaning down to kiss me once more, he tastes of mint and something distinctly Hale. His tongue sweeps past my parted lips and I open for him, my own tongue desperate to lick against his. My hips push closer toward his hand where he's still treating me to light caresses over my panties.

I reach for him, gripping the hard ridge in his pants, and he releases a strangled grunt.

"Not yet." Lifting my hand away from his happy place, he places it on the bed beside me and intertwines our fingers, holding me there while his other hand continues its magic against me.

The knowledge that he's hard and wants me as badly as I want him is a powerful thing. He's so much bigger than any man I've seen before, and I can't wait to feel him inside me. My body aches for it. Yet, he's so in control of everything—of my pleasure and of his own restraint. I want him naked and on top of me, but it seems for now, he wants to torture me.

"I need you to understand something. A basic concept." With a single kiss placed just below my ear, he pulls back, looking down at where his fingers are still rubbing against me. "Men are visual creatures. And even though you think these plain white panties aren't sexy…there's a tiny damp spot I can see right here."

He rubs his thumb over my clit again, and I release a shuddering breath.

"That is sexy as fuck." His voice is rough, aroused.

"Hale…" I groan, becoming increasingly frustrated with his fingers teasing between my thighs.

His pupils dilate when I moan his name, and just when I think I can't take any more of his slow torture, he moves my panties to the side. Sliding his fingers along the seam of my sex, he parts me and sinks two fingers deep inside.

My hips lift off the bed and a groan of satisfaction falls from my mouth. "Yes, please," I beg.

"Even when you don't think you're sexy, move with confidence. When you own it, when you work with what you've got, it will always be a turn-on."

Understanding that this is part of his lesson, my sluggish brain eventually catches on to what he's saying.

"So, you mean I could do this…" I move my hand between my legs and my index finger begins slowly circling my clit while his fingers slide in and out of me. "…and it would be sexy."

He makes a hungry noise in his throat and my pulse riots. "Fuck yeah, it is. Move with confidence. Remember that."

I close my eyes and let my head fell back onto the pillow as I get lost in the sensations. He thrusts his fingers upward, stroking my G-spot, and I begin climbing toward orgasm almost immediately. A few more strokes and I'm clenching down on his fingers, an intense orgasm ripping through me. Blinding white light crashes over me as his fingers slowly withdraw.

"Wow. That was…" I struggle to catch my breath.

Hale leans over me and kisses the side of my neck. "You seem to be catching on to my lessons nicely." He nips at the tender skin at the base of my throat, and I realize he's nowhere near done with me. "Do you need a moment to recover?" His gaze moves between my breasts and my eyes.

I shake my head, the quiet intensity of the moment settling in. The flickering candlelight. The scent of my arousal in the air. I'm lost to him and this moment entirely, and I want more.

Hale rises from the bed and pulls his shirt over his head. His jeans and boxers go next, and he stands before me, completely nude, looking like a sexy, muscled god with his six-pack abs, his smooth and defined pecs, and impressive erection.

My eyes are drawn to it, and I don't even try not to stare. My greedy gaze drinks its fill. He's nicely manicured down there, and his cock is long, thick, and straight. It's perfect, actually, and I've never thought that about a penis before. His fist closes around it, and he strokes himself once from base to tip.

"Do you want me to fuck you, peach?" he whispers.

More than anything. "Yes," I answer dutifully.

He moves onto the bed, kneeling between my parted knees. There is not even a question of protection, both of us having disclosed our personal health records, including the fact that I'm on birth control.

I've never been so crazed with want and lust that I've felt out of control, but that's how he makes me feel. I hate his practiced restraint and composure. He slowly slides the panties down my legs and discards them at the end of the bed.

Leaning over me, Hale brings my hands up above my head, linking our fingers and pressing me firmly into the bed. His hard arousal presses against my center, and I want to rock against him, to angle my hips and force him inside, but I don't. He kisses me deeply and I follow his lead, my lips parting and my tongue dancing with his.

He is by far the best kisser I've ever had the pleasure of kissing. His lips are soft, yet firm, his tongue warm and delivering subtle strokes that leave me wanting more. More of everything. I imagine what his mouth would feel like between my legs.

Unable to hold back, I grind against him and he groans. "Not yet." He pulls his lips from mine. "I don't want to hurt you with this." He slides his cock against my slickness. "Need to make sure you're ready, okay?"

I'm about to tell him I'm ready when his mouth lowers to my breasts and his tongue licks a path between my cleavage.

"I want to fuck these later," he murmurs. "They're gorgeous."

I've always hated that my breasts were on the smaller side, but the way Hale is worshipping them changes my mind. I feel perfectly whole in his presence. He holds nothing back, releasing my hands to push my breasts together and lick the cleavage he creates, sucking firmly on my nipples until I'm about to scream. I reach between us, gripping his solid cock, and slide my hand up and down.

He sucks in a breath and curses softly. "You better be ready for this."

"I am," I pant, squeezing him.

"I'm going to tell you exactly what to do. Do you understand?"

My gaze lifts to his and I nod.

Taking his thick cock in his hand, he strokes himself slowly again. *Is he doing that just to torture me?*

"A man likes it when you know how to please him. You're going to become the girl he can't live without. The only girl he wants to fuck. Period."

I stare at him, incredulous, wondering how exactly I'm going to accomplish that.

"Turn over. Put that nice round ass in the air. Just like before."

I roll onto my stomach and then lift my behind up, curling my knees under me. My cheek rests on the pillow, and though I can't see much, I can see enough. Hale rises up on his knees behind me, admiring the view and positioning himself against me.

He trails his finger down my spine, not stopping until I feel his finger between my cheeks, ghosting over me. "Did I tell you already that I want to fuck you here?" He gives my butt a quick swat, and I release a grunt.

"Y-yes." I don't think that's on tonight's agenda, but he constantly keeps me guessing, so who knows. I am totally at his mercy, and I'd be lying if I said I didn't like it.

Palming both of my ass cheeks in his large hands, he aligns his eager cock against me and thrusts forward. My pussy squeezes around him, not quite as ready for the invasion as I thought. I'm instantly reminded that I've been celibate for four long years.

He stills against me. "Relax your muscles, okay?" His tone is sincere and soft, and I'm starting to crave this tender side of him that he only shows on occasion.

I take a deep breath and when I exhale, he pushes forward again, sinking a little deeper this time. *Dear God.* He's stretching me in the most wonderful way, easing in and pulling back slowly, carefully. The competent way he moves speaks to his experience with women, something I don't want to think about in this moment.

"Goddamn, you're tight, peach." His voice comes out strained and raw.

One more long, slow thrust and finally he's buried fully within me. A low moan escapes my lips. Ever since our first meeting, I've imagined what fucking him would be like. Never in my dirtiest fantasy was it this good. He moves in and out at the perfect pace. Varying his thrusts from hard and fast to deep and slow, lingering when he's fully buried inside me as if he wants to savor the feeling. The way his hands grip my hips, and he pulls me back firmly against him with each thrust, tells me I'm going to have little fingertip bruises there tomorrow. And damn if I don't love the thought of him marking me.

"Fuck me back, sweetheart. Get into it and let yourself go. A man needs to know he can get you so full of need that you have no choice but to rock these beautiful hips closer and take every last inch of what he's giving you."

Hale's movements still, giving me the chance to practice taking the lead. It feels so foreign to me, so new, that for a moment, I struggle to find a rhythm that will suit us both, my body stopping altogether.

"You're thinking too much," he says, leaning over me and pressing a single kiss between my shoulder blades. "Just feel. Get rid of all those voices in your head. Let everything go and simply feel. It's just me and you, and we can practice for as long as you need to."

Closing my eyes, I take a deep breath. Embracing my inner sex kitten, I imagine what the view must be like for him. Me in a position of complete surrender, my ass on display, his cock impaling me, owning me. It's an erotic sight. I push my butt back, sliding on his cock until his heavy balls slap against me, and he grunts out a sound of delicious pleasure.

I try the move again, withdrawing and rocking back, wiggling my butt in a way I hope is enticing. But I believe him—this is a judgment-free zone, and that thought alone provides confidence. Knowing I can try things I've never been brave enough to try is freeing.

He places one hand flat on my lower back, but he lets me do all the work, and I practice rocking back and forth on him.

He shudders, then whispers a curse.

"How is it?" I ask, glancing back at him, suddenly needing some reassurance.

"Uh, you're doing good." His voice is impossibly tight, and something tells me I'm doing better than *good.*

Deep satisfaction rises inside me and I let go, fucking him faster, pushing my ass back to take him deep again and again. The unintended consequence is that I stop thinking so much and just *feel.* It's incredible, and soon I feel my release building.

"Hale…" I cry out. "I'm close…"

Suddenly he pulls free and my body mourns his loss, but only for a second. Before I know it, I'm tugged up from the bed, wrapped in his strong arms, and laid back down—on my back this time. And then the broad head of him is pushing into me again, claiming me.

"I want to watch you when you come." He thrusts forward and this time, I don't wait to be told; my hips lift from the bed and I meet him thrust for thrust.

God, we're quite a sight. His huge, thick cock parting me, sinking deep within my pink, tender flesh. My pelvis rocking against his. Our hands locked together. Our eyes lifting to each other's.

"Come all over my dick, baby. Just like that," he growls, his eyes glued to the spot where his body is joined with mine.

I fall apart, climaxing almost immediately, moaning his name in a litany of mumbled cries.

His chest shudders and he lets go, the warmth of his semen marking me all along my stomach and thighs as he pulls out at the last second and strokes himself in the most sensual way.

Moments later he moves from the bed, and I hear his footsteps in the hall. He returns with a warm cloth that he uses to clean me. I wonder if this is all part of the service, but the look in his eyes is pure adoration, and I'm lost to him. I've never been so thoroughly worshipped, taken, and now his kindness feels like too much.

"That was perfect," he says, breathless, kissing my temple once again.

A thousand emotions slam into me at once. *Pleasure. Desire. Fear. Disgust.*

I am the definition of a hot mess. With my hair clinging to my damp skin, and my lungs still heaving from my powerful release, I feel lost and broken. I curl onto my side and hug my arms around my body, hating that he's about to see me cry.

I'm supposed to be doing this because I want to date Kirby. Right now, he's the furthest thing from my mind, and I want nothing more than Hale to take me in his arms and never let me go.

"Hey, hey…" The softness of his voice startles me. "What's wrong?" He strokes my hair, running his fingers against my scalp and through the length of my hair.

I can't answer at first. Tears roll down my cheeks for reasons unknown as feelings of deep regret and sadness wash over me. I have no idea what's gotten into me.

Hale leans over me with a pained expression, opening my legs and inspecting me carefully. "Did I hurt you?"

"No. No, nothing like that." I take a deep breath and wipe my eyes. "I'm sorry, it's stupid."

"Tell me what you're feeling right now."

I'm feeling confused and... I don't even know how to explain it. Was that as intense for him as it was for me? Probably not. His face gives nothing away, and his calm demeanor makes me feel unnerved, inferior. I'm nothing more than a client; this is just sex to him. To me, it was the most powerful, incredible thing I've ever experienced, but to him I'm merely another appointment in his date book. How do I tell him that without sounding totally crazy?

"I'm not sure," I say.

"The sex between us was intense," he says as though he's plucked the words right from my brain.

"Yeah," I agree.

"So intense that sometimes it can become confused with something it's not—something more emotional. It's a powerful thing, submitting like that, giving yourself to me the way you did. Have you done anything like that with a man before?"

"No. I... That was a first for me." I felt wild and uninhibited, and I let myself go in front of him like I've never done before.

"I thought so." He strokes my hair again, the look of pride in his eyes as he watches me makes me aware that I'd do it all over again—anything he asks and more. "But we can't confuse what this is," he says, bringing me back to the moment. "It's just physical." The strained way he says it makes me wonder who he's trying to convince—me or him.

He tugs me down against him and curls his body around me as he tells me to just breathe, and I do. As I try to get my emotions under control, he holds me and assures me my reaction is normal.

"Remember when we talked about aftercare?" he asks, still holding me.

"Yes." I never dreamed I would be in a position to need it, remembering how hysterical his friend Chrissy was, sobbing and sounding desperate as he coached her through her meltdown. I've never been like that after sex, but this felt like a lot more than just sex.

"We didn't talk about sub drop, but I think we should. Submitting can be an emotional experience. After a scene, your adrenaline and all the other chemicals that your body naturally produces are at an all-time high. When they crash, it can leave you feeling sad, lonely, and confused. The more intense the scene, the more intense the drop can be."

Listening to him talk, I feel relieved. It's nothing but my out-of-control hormones and emotions playing tricks on me. I focus on relaxing and clearing my mind. Listening to the sounds of his heartbeat, I enjoy the way his hands knead my muscles.

I have a choice to make. I can enjoy every minute of his attention, every gift he has to offer, or I can go it alone. Why wouldn't I want his help?

Convincing myself to relax, I'm soon warm and comfortable and feeling drowsy. Everything is going to be okay. I think. He murmurs calming words, praises me for tonight, and continues stroking my hair and my skin.

I've let him in so completely, and hate that I don't know him better. "Will you tell me about your nana?" I ask softly, curious about this dominating man's soft side that I've only caught glimpses of.

"What do you want to know?" His tone is guarded as if he doesn't enjoy dishing out personal details.

I shrug. "I don't know. I'm curious, I guess. Are you close?"

He nods. "Other than my younger sister, she's the closest thing I have to family. She's put up with a lot of shit from me over the years, and now I take care of her."

"What's she like?" I try to picture Hale hanging around a little old lady, and fail miserably. I'd have an easier time picturing him in a BDSM dungeon, clad in black leather, with a sub tied up in intricate knots.

"She's an eighty-year-old who makes the best goddamn blueberry pie in the world, likes to knit me hideous sweaters, and continually asks me when I'm going to settle down."

I giggle, picturing the intrusion, because I really can't imagine anyone questioning him. "And what do you tell her?"

"Never." His voice is flat, convincing me he's serious. He has no interest in marriage or monogamy. The memory of overhearing those two women discussing his tragic past jumps into my brain, and I feel bad for him. It's a thought that makes me want to take him in my arms and hold him close, but somehow I know he wouldn't allow that.

After a few minutes, Hale gets up, blows out his candle, and dresses. I watch the way the muscles in his broad shoulders move, the tone and definition of his firm thighs as he pulls on his jeans. He's really quite gorgeous.

A passing thought makes my stomach sink, and I realize this could all be a terrible combination. His overwhelming masculine presence, my desperate need for love…

Am I headed straight for disaster?

Chapter Twelve

HALE

It's Sunday, which means I'm sitting in a damp-smelling nursing-home room with Nana. Yet no matter how hard I try, I can't seem to forget my last session with Brielle, my sexy little peach.

Every detail is seared into my memory. Her tight little ass working against me. *Fuck*. Her petite body latching onto mine, milking me to the last drop. I could quickly see her becoming an addiction. One I wasn't allowed to overdose on, as much as I might want to. I had a job to do. That was it.

Nana waves her index finger at me. "Grab me my knitting bag out of the closet. I made you something."

I have an entire dresser full of hideous sweaters, knitted caps, and misshapen scarves courtesy of Nana. If I'm ever invited to an ugly-Christmas-sweater party, I'm fairly certain I could go dressed from head to toe in colorful, itchy wool.

I grab the bag and hand it to her. She produces a royal purple turtleneck vest thingy and hands it to me with a proud grin.

"Wow. It's just…I'm speechless. Thank you, Nana."

Dear God, this thing needs to be burned. But hell, it gives her something to do, and gives the dresser in my spare room a purpose. Everyone wins.

"Put it on. I need to make sure it fits."

I hold it up to myself. "Oh, it'll fit."

Satisfied, she smiles, and I return to the armchair next to her.

I was seventeen when my parents were killed in a plane crash during their dream vacation to Alaska. It was a small bush plane, used for the excursion fishing trip my dad talked about for months.

Nanette—Nana—was a member of the church they attended. I went only on major holidays and had met her once or twice. I didn't really know her and she didn't know me. But she stepped up and claimed ownership for me, along with my younger sister, Macey.

Seventy years old and a devoted Christian, Nana and I were an unlikely combination. I remember the first time I laid eyes on her at the funeral. Her skin was the color of coffee, and her braided hair was a mixture of salt and pepper. She came right up to me—we were the only two not crying—and as she stood by my side, she leaned toward me and said in a low voice that crying wasn't going to bring them back. I nodded in agreement and watched as their caskets were lowered into the ground. I felt numb. Empty. And all cried out.

From that moment on, I liked her. I liked her strength and her character. But when she petitioned the state to grant her custody rather than have us go into foster care, it shocked the shit out of me.

She got her way. Macey and I lived with Nana through high school. During college and then in law school, I always had a place with her at holidays and breaks. Last year she was moved into an assisted living home. For many years she took care of me, and now I take care of her. It's the least I can do. She's family now.

The afternoon nurse—Trisha, I think—comes in with a tray with Nana's meds. Something for her blood pressure, and something to help her go to the bathroom. She's healthy as a damn horse, thank God. Trisha bends over to set down the tray, and pushes her ample cleavage into my face.

Hello there.

Once she's gone, Nana rolls her eyes at the overeager nurse. "That hussy needs to slow down. She's on you like stink on an ape. A man likes to chase a woman, not the other way around. You don't want to be smothered, do you?"

"By her?" I grin crookedly. "Might not be so bad."

"You're wicked."

"In all the best ways," I assure her.

She laughs, but soon her smile fades and her expression turns more serious. "When are you going to settle down, Cameron? I'd like to see you with a nice girl. I won't be around forever. I am eighty-one this year, you know?"

I swallow, hating that her age is something we even have to think about. She's all I have left. Along with Macey, who I don't see nearly enough now that she moved. "I know, Nana. I'm already planning a big surprise party."

"It's not a surprise if I know about it." She raises one penciled-on eyebrow.

"I wouldn't want to be responsible for a heart attack, or bladder failure, or whatever." I grin at her.

"Wicked," she says again.

I'm not sure how long I can keep dodging her questions about my future, but let's hope for a long, long time.

Chapter Thirteen

How in the fuck did I think this was a good idea? Never agree to sex with a good-looking, intelligent man with no hope of it leading to something.

It turns out I can't do it.

I can't separate sex from emotion. All day at work, my body is going through the motions, showing overpriced townhomes to eager couples, demonstrating the features like walk-in closets and electric cooktops while my mind runs rampant with thoughts of him.

Hale. His firm hands at my hips, his warm mouth on mine, the dark, hungry look in his eyes when he watches me. In his presence I feel alive and wanted, and it's becoming addictive. I don't know how I'm going to give him up in a few weeks. These are the terms I agreed to, so why do I feel like I'm being split in two?

My ringing cell captures my attention and I pull it from my purse.

It's Kirby.

My stomach sinks. Before I have time to analyze my body's reaction, I answer the call. "Hello?"

"Where ya been hiding, ladybug?" he asks with his playful chuckle that instantly sets me at ease.

"I—I don't know." I realize I've been spending all my free time with Hale, and when I'm not with him, his commanding, masculine presence dominates my thoughts. This whole thing is supposed to be about Kirby, and I've barely given him a passing thought the past two weeks.

"Well first, we need to make plans to hang out. And second, I'm thinking of buying a place. I need your real estate expertise. Think you could show me some condos?"

"That's awesome, Kirby. Of course I'll help you."

"Cool. This weekend work for you?"

"Um..." I hesitate, my mind darting to Hale. We haven't arranged our next lesson, but knowing they usually happen on the weekend, I don't want to commit to plans with Kirby yet. "Can I get back to you on that?"

"'Course," he says.

I'm trying to fit my plans for Kirby around my schedule with Hale. It should probably be the other way around, but I don't care.

God, what is wrong with me? One night of great sex shouldn't negate five years of unrequited love. I wasn't thinking clearly. It must be that sub-drop thingy Hale explained to me. That's all. I need to enjoy this time and my lessons with him. Ride the wave, so to speak, and whatever other body parts he'll allow. Because, dear God in heaven, the man fucks like a wildcat.

"Just text me when you know your schedule," Kirby says, pulling my mind from the gutter.

"Absolutely," I tell him.

I hang up and check the time before stuffing my cell phone into my purse. I'm due at a brand new condo complex in the heart of the city in less than twenty minutes. It'll be a small miracle if I make it on time.

Somehow I make it just on time, using the digital keypad on the front door to let myself in and turn on all the lights before my clients arrive.

City View Condominiums is a new building that's still under construction, but their model is beautifully finished and staged with elegant furniture and art. I turn on the lamp in the living room and flip on the gas fireplace.

Satisfied that everything looks perfect, I pull the brochure from my file folder and wait for my clients. It would be amazing to sell one of these condos today. The commission on a half-million dollar property would make my bank account happy.

A light knock on the door signals their arrival.

"You guys made it," I say, pulling open the door in a way I hope is inviting. "Welcome to City View."

I've been working with Mark and Sarah for about three weeks now. We've toured high-end apartments and luxury condos all over the city, but this is by far the nicest place I've shown them. It's a bit over their budget, but I'm pretty sure they're going to love it. After all, I love it. I'd love to live here.

"Wow, this is gorgeous," Sarah says as we enter the kitchen and take note of the granite countertops, glass-mosaic-tiled backsplash, and stainless-steel appliances.

"Each owner is able to customize their unit, choosing flooring, counters, and paint colors," I tell them.

They seem impressed as we wander from room to room. When we enter the master bedroom, they stand at the floor-to-ceiling windows, admiring the city views the building was named for.

My cell phone begins ringing and I fish it from my purse.

It's Hale. He's probably calling to arrange our next lesson, and once I find out the date, I can text Kirby back.

"If you'll excuse me for a moment," I say, holding up my cell like it's some urgent business call. I step into the spacious master bath, since this should only take a minute.

"Hello?"

"Peach," he says, his deep voice rumbling along my skin as if he's right here in the room with me.

"Hi."

"Where are you?"

"I'm showing some clients the model at City View Condos. Why?"

"I'm in the mood for lesson number three."

My belly tightens. "When are you thinking?" I peek out into the master bedroom to see Mark and Sarah have moved over to inspect the walk-in closet with its various shelves, drawers, and compartments.

"Right now. Remember when I told you I was going to push you, test your limits."

"Yes," I say, my brow crinkling. I'm unsure what he's getting at.

"This is a test, my peach. I want you to touch yourself, make yourself come while I listen."

My mouth falls open. He can't be serious. "I'm showing a home to clients. They'll hear me."

"Not if you're quiet."

I pause, glancing up into the mirror. This is crazy. Completely insane. So why is my heart pounding like a drum and my body thrumming with eager anticipation? I pace the small room from one end to the other, trying to form a coherent argument on why this is a bad idea.

"Tell me exactly where you are," Hale says.

"A bathroom."

"Is there a mirror?"

"Yes." I glance up and find my reflection. My flushed skin feels hot, and my nipples harden beneath my form-fitting button-down top.

"Good. I want you to slip your hand into the front of your panties and tell me how good it feels."

"I can't," I say softly.

"Brielle." His tone is firm, and a pang of regret hits me. I don't like disappointing this man. "Would it help if you knew I had my cock in my hand, and it's rock hard and aching? All I can think about is your tight little cunt squeezing me."

My body clenches at his words. It shouldn't, but the luxurious opulence of the bathroom is inviting. If Hale were here, he'd lift me onto the marble counter, push my skirt up my thighs, and fuck me hard and fast while I held on to his solid biceps and shoulders. It's an enticing thought.

"I do miss your cock," I admit softly.

He makes a small sound of approval, and I'm urged on. This is wicked and naughty and so very wrong, but I don't care.

I glance out one last time. My clients are admiring the built-in cabinets on the far wall.

"Brielle?" Hale groans, the need evident in his voice.

I want to please him. I want the release that would come with touching myself, but at the last moment, sanity steps in. There's no way I can do this. But I know refusing him would be a bad idea. I turn on my most sultry voice and whisper, "Oh, that feels good."

I hope he can't tell I'm completely faking it. I open the door and peek out at Matt and Sarah, and give them the thumbs-up sign.

"That's a good girl," he says softly, clearly pleased with my performance. "I want you to take a picture of your wet pussy with your fingers buried inside, and text it to me."

"What are the monthly association fees for this building?" Sarah asks, wandering closer.

"What the fuck was that?" Hale asks, obviously pissed off at my little performance.

"Um, I have to go," I squeak out and hang up the phone.

With my heart slamming erratically against my ribs and my face flushed, I do my best to complete the tour, showing off all the features of the unit, then cover the community features and association costs.

Their interest is obvious, and Sarah squeezes her husband's hand under the table as if to say, *this is the one.*

A knock at the door interrupts us and I excuse myself to answer it, wondering if the agency double-booked a showing today.

When I open the door, Hale strides inside as if he owns the place, dressed in a navy suit, crisp shirt, and striped tie.

"Are you almost through?" he asks, gliding past me without so much as a hello or explanation.

"Uh…yes," I manage, trailing after him as quickly as my high heels will allow.

He stops at the dining table where my clients are seated. "Thank you for coming today. If you could see yourselves out, Brielle will be in touch later this afternoon."

They share a confused look, but Sarah shrugs. "Okay, we'll talk later."

My professionalism returning, I follow them to the door, handing them the packet of information I prepared. "Thank you for coming. I think City View has everything you guys have been looking for. I'll be in touch."

As soon as the door closes, I spin on my heel to face Hale, hot anger rising up inside me. "This is my job! You can't just show up like this."

He stalks closer, his dark eyes pinned on mine, and doesn't stop until my back is pressed against the wall. "We had an agreement. I told you that I would push you outside of your comfort zone, test you and challenge you. I didn't force this arrangement on you. You agreed, heartily. I'm only following through with my end of the deal."

I'm about to ask him how he knew where I was, and then I remember that I told him when he called. My anger subsides just a fraction. I was pretty much through with my meeting anyway, and based on my clients' reaction to seeing the drop-dead gorgeous man in front of me, there's been no real harm done.

"You need to be punished for that little stunt you pulled earlier. Making my dick hard and swollen like that…" He makes a grunting sound of disapproval, and my pulse spikes. I can read the need written all over his features, in his tight posture. The need to punish me is flaring inside him, and that excites the fuck out of me. *What's happening to me?*

"I'm sorry, sir." I blink up at him, my eyes communicating my own need.

"What should we do to settle this?" His firm hands settle on my waist, making my belly twist with nerves.

Boldly, I reach down between us, my hand curling around the weight of his shaft, that even soft, is heavy in my hand. "I could take care of this," I offer.

His eyes sink closed for a moment, and I feel him begin to harden against my palm. When he opens his eyes again, his perfect control is back. "Would you like that, pet?"

I nod. "Yes." The idea of sinking to my knees before him and taking his heavy cock in my mouth makes me wet.

He shakes his head, telling me I've said the wrong thing, given too much away. "Not this time," he says, then reaches for my throat.

Lightly circling his fingers around my neck, his lips graze mine. With his hands at my throat, holding me in place, he has my full attention, which I think is the entire point. His thumb strokes along the column of my neck, and he smiles slightly when he feels the insistent thrum of my pulse.

"Being in trouble excites you. Naughty girl," he remarks.

I make a small whimpering sound as the need to touch him, to kiss him, rises inside me. The masculine scent of his skin, the way he towers over me, even in my high-heeled shoes, the devastating look that says *you will belong to my cock*. It's all too much.

"How much time do I have before I have to return you?" he asks.

I can see into the kitchen, to the clock on the wall. "I have forty-five minutes before my next appointment."

"Perfect." Placing a kiss at the base of my throat, Hale steps back and begins removing his tie as I watch in hungry anticipation the way he slides the knot free and pulls it from his collar. "Turn around."

I spin around so I'm facing the wall, and Hale takes each of my wrists, binding them together firmly with his silk tie. He's silent, and I can't even begin to guess at his emotions. Once I'm secured, he guides me by my shoulders farther into the condo, my feet carrying me blindly down the hall. He leads me into the master bathroom where I was earlier, and faces us at the mirror with him standing behind me.

His rugged jawline is sporting a five o'clock shadow, and he looks devastatingly handsome. He could easily pass for a movie star on the cover of *People Magazine*'s "Sexiest Man Alive" issue. His eyes are glued to me, just like mine are to him.

I watch in the mirror as his deft fingers make quick work of unbuttoning my shirt, revealing the white lacy bra underneath.

"Just as I thought." He traces his thumbs over my already hardened nipples. They're swollen and ultra-sensitive with the rasp of the lace between us. My breath gets caught in my throat, and I moan softly as the sensations tumble through me.

After flicking open the front clasp of my bra to allow my breasts to tumble free, Hale picks me up and sets me down on the countertop, much like I fantasized about earlier. He brings his mouth to one breast, firmly sucking my nipple into his warm mouth, making me cry out.

I want to touch him, to stroke him, but with my hands tied behind my back, all I can do is sit perched before him, taking every ounce of pleasure he so expertly delivers. He moves from one breast to the other, licking and sucking until I'm soaking wet and about to explode with need.

When he rises to his full height before me, his lips are soft and damp from his onslaught of naughty kisses, and I want nothing more than those lips on mine. But Hale reaches into his jacket pocket and withdraws a small silver bullet-shaped vibrator. With a twist to the end, it hums to life, and butterflies take flight in my stomach.

Hale looks down at the toy buzzing in his hand and then back up at me with a devious glint in his eyes. "Now, what should we do with this?"

I'm practically squirming on the countertop. He can read me like a book. He knows I want to feel the buzz of the toy against me. But trying to maintain my composure, even with my hands tied behind my back and my bare breasts thrust out, I lift my chin. "Do you always carry a vibrator around in your suit jacket?"

"When I'm working with bad little girls who need to be fucked? Yes."

My eyebrows dart up as my bravado fades away. "It seems you've thought of everything."

"I told you I'm the best."

His tone is confident, sure, direct. He is at his most beautiful when he's like this. Tall. Commanding. In charge. I like it way more than I ever dreamed I would.

"Have you ever used a toy like this, Brielle?"

I've used a vibrator before; I'm not *that* innocent. "Yes," I murmur.

His jaw twitches. "But have you used it here?"

He places the toy against my nipple, which hardens instantly as unexpected pleasure jolts through me. The sensation is like nothing I've ever felt. Warm, delicious heat builds as the toy hums against my sensitive skin. He circles one nipple and then the other, watching as my chest heaves. Desire coils tightly inside me, and my body silently screams for a release.

"How does that feel, pet?" he asks, his tone low and sultry, and his eyes glued to my breasts.

"G-good," I manage.

"Hmm. Just good?"

I meet his intense stare, watching, waiting to see what he'll do next.

His hand, along with the toy disappears under my skirt, and seconds later I feel the vibration against my panties. He moves the toy back and forth over me, and the warm pulses push my pleasure to its limits. My hips move on their own, writhing, rocking to get closer.

"And how about this?"

"Oh God," I moan.

He presses the toy right against my clit, and I immediately build toward climax.

"Don't come. Do you understand me?" Hale says.

I moan, a tiny cry bubbling in my throat. There's no way I can hold back, but I nod my head.

"Good girl."

With his free hand, he unlatches his belt, reaches inside his pants, and pulls out his already erect cock. While still stimulating me, he strokes himself up and down his long shaft. My gaze is glued to him. He's so open, so free with his body, so sexually confident. It's a huge turn-on.

The buzzing between my thighs pushes me closer and closer toward release, and I bite down on my lower lip, crying out in a mix of pleasure and pain at holding it back.

"Hale," I pant, desperate for more.

He turns off the toy and helps me down from the counter. I'm reeling from our encounter and struggling to process what comes next. Soon, I'm on the floor between his feet, looking up at him when I realize the front door is still unlocked, and someone could come in at any time. The secret thrill of being discovered only excites me more. My breath comes in ragged pants; I'm so needy and desperate for more.

Hale pulls my blouse open, then slides it along with my bra down my shoulders so my chest is fully exposed. He palms my breasts in his hands, pushing them together to create ample cleavage. The little toy has disappeared back inside his pocket, and I mourn its loss.

He runs his cock along the valley of my breasts, and his chest shudders with a sharp inhale.

"Fuck. No lube. I guess I haven't thought of everything." He holds his palm in front of my mouth. "Spit," he commands.

I do, wetting his palm with a drop of saliva.

He coats his cock in the moisture and then slides it between my breasts. He moves with controlled thrusts, his cock, as hard as stone, plunging into the space between my breasts. It's highly erotic watching him, and I'm transfixed. All but for the tick in his jaw and the pulse thrumming in his neck, you'd never know he was about to lose control.

"Fucking hell," he groans and takes his cock in his hand. After a few uneven strokes, his warm come is decorating my breasts, dripping onto my nipples, and covering my chest. He moans my name and my pussy tightens, clenching as a rush of endorphins hit my system.

I've never done anything even remotely like this—a midday romp at a model home—where anyone could come waltzing in. But it seems with this man, I'm not myself. I'm no longer boring, hardworking, bookworm Brie. I'm someone sexy, wanton, daring, and spontaneous. I fucking love it.

Hale helps me to my feet and turns on the water, warming it before wiping me clean with handfuls of toilet paper.

He unties my wrists and I stretch them, the loss of blood flow making my hands tingly and cool to the touch. He lifts each to his mouth, pressing soft kisses to my palms and the underside of each wrist, inspecting each hand carefully.

His dark eyes latch onto mine. "Are you okay?"

I nod. "I'm fine. A little sexually frustrated, but I'll live." I smile, trying to convey that my wrists really are fine.

"Today was about teaching you a lesson."

"I know," I say demurely.

"You did very well." He kisses my lips once, softly, and I immediately lean into him, wanting more. He chuckles against my mouth. "Next time," he promises.

Next time. Such beautiful words. I'm already anticipating it way more than I should.

Chapter Fourteen

HALE

My encounter earlier with Brielle is still buzzing in my mind. What the fuck was I thinking? Marking her that way? She isn't mine. Yet I fucked her tits, let go completely, and emptied myself right over her pounding heart. It was all I could do to clean up and flee that condo before I tied her to the bed and fucked her for hours.

All of this is going to come crashing down around me when we're through. I know that, and yet I feel powerless to end it.

Later I find myself at the grocery store, wandering the aisles, absentmindedly throwing things into my basket. I make three loops around the store, forgetting the reason I've come, when I find myself staring blankly at a display of peaches. I can't stop myself from thinking about Brielle's soft, creamy skin, the eager way she blinked up at me, ready to please me, the pleasure I felt at taking her to new heights. Watching her open herself up to me is like witnessing a beautiful awakening. It's fucking addictive. This isn't her world, yet she's so willing to go on this journey with me. *For me.*

I hated withholding her orgasm earlier, and not just because she's so beautiful when she comes. I've never cared before, never felt the deep anguish that comes after, never felt so incomplete parting ways with a client before.

Orgasm denial is a pretty standard punishment. Yet using it with Brielle felt like part of me had died. That's some sick shit right there. I'm certain if Reece heard all these inner thoughts, he'd fucking neuter me on the spot. I'm supposed to be the one teaching her, yet I feel as if I'm learning all kinds of new things about myself.

Picking up a ripe, plump peach, I bring it to my nose and inhale. The sweet, succulent fruit is nowhere near as fragrant as Brielle, but I add it to my basket all the same.

I'm grooming her for Kirby. I repeat that mantra in my head as I head to the checkout.

Later, I pay a surprise visit to Nana, who watches me with guarded eyes, proclaiming that there's something different about me. She knows it, I know it, yet neither of us knows exactly what it is.

"Is there a woman in your life?" she asks as I'm putting on my jacket to leave for home.

I kiss her on the head and hand her a peach. "Good night, Nana."

Chapter Fifteen

BRIELLE

Have you ever been near someone where the chemistry was so powerful you had to physically restrain yourself? I could easily get lost in Hale's gaze, his sultry remarks, and masculine confidence. I could spend hours just staring into the depths of his dark eyes. I could turn over my heart, my body, and let him take the lead. But I know in doing so, I'd lose myself completely.

And after my midday meet-up with Hale, I'm more confused than ever. The things I feel when I'm with him go way beyond what a student-mentor relationship should.

Deciding I need some girl time to clear my head, as well as a large margarita, I dial Julie.

Soon we're at The Lettuce Leaf, a favorite dinner spot of ours. They make the most insanely awesome organic peach margaritas, and Julie is grilling me about Hale. Of course, I haven't told her his name; it doesn't seem right sharing that tidbit of information.

"You've got to give me more than *that*," she says, rolling her eyes at me.

"We had sex, okay?" I whisper. It felt like *a lot more* than just sex, but I don't know how to put into words what I experienced last Saturday night. Or again today while at the model home. I'm learning so many things about myself, about sex. Sex itself is nice, but couple it with a powerful connection, and several intense orgasms, and it becomes life changing.

"And? How was it? Was he worth the money?"

I cringe. She makes it sound like I've hired a prostitute, which I basically have, but *sheesh*, it's not something I want to be reminded of. He's a sexual mentor; there's a difference.

Julie's expression turns sheepish as I glance around at the people seated near us. "Sorry."

"It was…he was…" I chew on my lip.

He was amazing, but here's the thing—of course he was. I hired him as a sexual guide and teacher, and he delivered. It's as simple as that. He's paid quite well to do what he does; it wasn't due to some inexplicable connection we share.

"It was exactly as it should be, I guess. Eye-opening and worth every last penny."

She smiles, satisfied. "That's my girl." She raises her margarita glass, clinking it to mine.

I don't feel like anyone's girl. I feel like drowning my sorrows in cheap liquor and decisions I'll regret in the morning.

"What are we doing after this?" I say around a mouthful of guacamole. "I feel like dancing."

Julie smiles. "That can be arranged. Let's go to that new nightclub, Dazzle."

After a stop at my apartment where we primp, reapply our makeup, and search my closet for the tiniest outfits we can find, we set off for Dazzle.

Three vodka-cranberry cocktails later and I'm on the dance floor, shaking what my mother blessed me with. I feel loose and carefree. *Hale who?*

Determined to force all thoughts of him and our arrangement from my mind, I bounce to the hip-hop beat, rocking my hips and shaking my ass in time to the music. Julie is chatting with an older guy at the bar, and wanting nothing to do with men tonight, I've ventured off alone in search of an ear-splitting beat that will obliterate all rational thought.

My phone vibrates against my hip, and I pull it out to see a text from Kirby. I left him hanging about this weekend. *Oops.* I guess I've been more distracted than I realized.

KIRBY: When are we hanging out? I need a Brie fix.

He's signed his text with a winking face, and my heart swells at his words. Maybe there is hope for us yet.

I reply with a smiley face of my own.

BRIELLE: How about this weekend? I'm at Dazzle getting drunk right now.

KIRBY: Long week?

BRIELLE: Something like that.

KIRBY: Let's hang out soon. I promise to cheer you up.

BRIELLE: Sounds good.

All at once, I feel better and more in control. If Hale's taught me anything, it's to let go of my self-consciousness and go with the flow. And right now, all I want is another cocktail, and the DJ to play that hip-hop song I love.

Lifting my hair off my neck in an attempt to cool down, I approach the bar and signal the bartender for another vodka cranberry. Soon, I'm stuffing a dollar into the tip jar and downing the bitter pink liquid in a long gulp.

When I feel a hand at my waist, I turn to find a man with messy dark hair and friendly blue eyes is smiling at me.

"I would offer you a drink, but I see you already have one."

I raise the glass. "Yes, I'm all set."

"How about a dance then?"

I open my mouth to refuse, but then the song I've been waiting to hear all night starts, and a surge of recklessness bubbles up inside me. I grab his hand, tugging him toward the dance floor.

Glancing back, I see him smile and set his beer down on a table as we pass. When we reach the center of the dance floor, I throw my hands up in the air and twist my body, dancing with my back to his front, wiggling against his groin and loving the way his hands skimming over my hips make me feel sexy and alive.

My mystery dance partner and I keep up our pace through three or four songs, until my bladder demands to be emptied. I lean in close to his ear, the intimacy of our dancing for the past fifteen minutes making me feel a false sense of comfort near him. Just as I'm about to whisper-shout that I need to use the restroom, a cool, firm grip latches onto my wrist and tugs me back into a broad male chest.

Black currant and sandalwood.

My body responds instantly, my nipples tightening in my bra, and chill bumps break out along my nape.

I turn and to come face-to-face with Hale, noting his features are twisted. He's mad, but I have no idea why.

"What are you doing here?" I shout over the music, not understanding how he knew where I was tonight. Or maybe it's nothing more than a coincidence, but a flicker of awareness claws at the back of my mind until the alcohol and the angry man in front of me trump it.

He curls one hand around mine and tugs me from the dance floor. We're heading for the back hallway and the bathrooms, thank God, so I don't protest.

Hale continues tugging me down the dimly lit hallway, past the restrooms and supply closets, until we're standing near the fire exit. I open my mouth to ask him what's wrong, when his mouth closes hot and hungry over mine.

He assaults me with passionate kisses, and all my questions die on my lips. Nothing matters right now except his touch. His hands slip under the edge of my shirt, tickling the flesh of my stomach, stopping just below the lace of my bra.

I'm immediately transported back to earlier today when he withheld my orgasm. My body, primed and ready, flexes toward his, my hips pushing forward until I feel his thick erection.

He bites my lower lip, barely enough to sting, and I can't help the moan that escapes at his rough contact. Then he pins me to the wall—hard—and my breath whooshes out of my lungs in a gasp.

"What the fuck do you think you're doing?" he asks, pulling his mouth from mine.

Me? He's the one who showed up here acting like a Neanderthal.

"What do you mean?" I ask, breathless.

"I denied your release earlier, and now you're out getting drunk at a nightclub, dancing with a man who'd happily take you home and fuck you. What am I supposed to think?"

His eyes are blazing on mine and his hair is messy and out of place, both indications he's out of control in a way I've never seen him before. I don't know if I love it or hate it.

My brain snaps into comprehension as all the puzzle pieces drop into place. "Are you jealous?"

His hand grips around my hip, and he squeezes. "You're supposed to be mine for the next six weeks."

"I am yours." The words have an undeniable truth to them that makes me feel like weeping. God, how did I allow myself to get so wrapped up in a man I can never have?

"Then let me ask you again, Brielle. What the fuck do you think you're doing?"

"I'm trying to get drunk and let loose. I'm sorry if you failed to notice, but this is fucking confusing." I gesture between me and him. The liquor has loosened my tongue, and I don't care. Suddenly, I want Hale to feel every bit as confused and out of control as I do.

He presses closer, his hips brushing mine as he asks, "What's confusing about it?" His mouth is mere inches from mine, his warm breath feathering over my lips.

"Why did you ask to kiss me that first night?" I whisper.

He's quiet for a moment while he watches my eyes as if he's contemplating how to answer. "I needed to see how you kissed. I needed to know if that was a skill we needed to work on together." His voice is composed and confident. But the pulse ticking in his throat, and the way his eyes strayed from mine when he answered...something feels off.

"I don't believe you."

"Why do you think I kissed you, Brielle?"

"Because you wanted to. Because you're just as attracted to me as I am to you."

"Does it matter?" he asks.

My heart is slamming against my ribs, hoping I'm about to discover he has secret feelings for me like I do for him.

"We both know this isn't headed anywhere. We like fucking each other. It's an added bonus to our lessons together. Don't read something into it that isn't there." His voice is whisper-soft, and his eyes are pleading with mine. I have no choice but to believe him.

Fuck.

The overwhelming urge to cry is back in full force. I want to understand why I haven't thought of Kirby once since Hale came into my life. I want to know why Hale puts up the wall that he does. I want to know where he works, what he likes for breakfast, and if he snores when he sleeps. I want to see him with his nana. The image of him helping a frail old lady up the steps to church makes me teary. And most of all, I want to understand how I've grown to be so desperately attached to him in such a short time.

"I have to pee," I say, breaking away from him and striding toward the restroom.

Once I've latched the stall door and covered the toilet seat with paper, I sink down and empty my bladder. Taking a deep breath, I ball the toilet paper in my fist.

My sessions with Hale creep into my mind. The first-time post-sex sub drop made me question everything. That was the best and most intense experience I've ever had with a man. Kirby was the furthest thing from my mind. And even in my buzzed state, I question if I can handle three more sessions. But how can I say no to the most beautifully brutal thing I've ever felt?

With absolute clarity, I realize that falling for Hale is a very real and terrifying possibility. And what will I do then? I certainly won't be okay with him mentoring and fucking the brains out of women all over Chicago. Besides, he's made it very clear that he and I do not have a future, so why am I sitting here dreaming of things that will never be?

Feeling somber and broken, I finish in the bathroom, taking a few moments to pull myself together before I go to find Hale.

He's waiting for me outside the ladies' restroom, looking solemn.

"Can I take you home?" he asks, his tone demanding.

My grand plans that included alcohol, dancing, and regret suddenly seem childish. "Yes."

I pull my phone from my purse to text Julie and tell her I'm leaving, when I see that she texted me fifteen minutes ago to tell me she was going home with the older guy she met at the bar. *Okay then.*

"Do you have a tab to settle?"

"No. I'm ready."

His hand on my lower back guides me to the exit, and I let him help me into the car.

We're both quiet on the drive to my place. The alcohol is starting to wear off, and I'm vaguely aware that I should be embarrassed that I practically admitted to feeling more for him than I should.

"Can I come in?" he asks, stopping the car on the street outside my building.

I should refuse him. That would be the logical thing to do. My current emotional state and growing feelings should signal that I need a breather from him—at least for the night.

Glancing over at him in the moonlit interior of the car, I see the ghost of a smile form on his lips as he says, "I left you hanging earlier. I can take care of that for you."

I don't know if this is a lesson or a mercy fuck, but I also know I won't refuse him. "Okay," I say, my voice flat.

He takes my chin in his hand and turns my head to meet his eyes. "I need a yes or no answer. Do you want me tonight?"

"Yes, I want you." There's so much truth in my words it hurts. I force a smile onto my lips.

Once we're inside, he lifts me into his arms and carries me to my bedroom. Carefully, he lays me down in the center of the bed, then removes my high heels, kissing the top of each naked foot. His lips are warm and soft, and send tingles rippling along my skin. He's being so tender, so sweet, I don't know what's gotten into him.

Slowly, methodically, he removes every stitch of clothing from my body, kissing me softly from head to toe. He's never been so attentive and careful like this with me before.

My head is spinning with questions, and I feel like I'm drowning in this big, beautiful man. I watch him in the moonlight, reveling in the feel of his rough stubble against my neck, breathing in his scent until I feel so full of him, I could burst. He's looking at me like I'm the beginning and ending of everything.

"Just feel," he whispers against my thigh.

I want to ask him what tonight's lesson is about, but I don't want to break the pleasurable spell he's cast over me. So I close my eyes and let the exquisite kisses he's placing just below my belly button push all the other noise from my brain.

Soon, he nudges my thighs apart, and I let my knees fall open to grant him the access he demands. There's no shyness, no self-consciousness with him. I want this so badly I can taste it. I want him to take me where only he can—where nothing exists but mindless pleasure, in that space where I shut off my brain and just feel, as he's commanded. It's a feeling I've grown to crave.

Warm, wet kisses placed delicately between my thighs make me gasp out loud and tug at his hair. He stops and pulls away, a smile on his lips, then goes to my dresser and searches the top drawer while I watch him, curious about what he could possibly be looking for. When he finds it, he strides confidently toward me and uses the black tights he's found to tie my wrists together above my head. I wonder if I've been pulling his hair too hard, or perhaps he simply likes seeing me tied up. He tugs his shirt off, and I'm treated to the smooth, muscular planes of his bare chest.

Before I can ponder his unique sexual preferences further, he lowers his mouth to my core once again and continues the punishing rhythm with his tongue that I know is going to make me come much faster than is ladylike.

My hips twist and my body trembles, cries claw their way up my throat, and still he doesn't relent. A powerful release pulls me under, and after what seems like an eternity, I emerge, breathless and disoriented.

"Holy hell," I mutter, closing my eyes and letting my head drop back onto the pillow.

Hale rises to his feet. "I'm not nearly done with you yet." His hands move to his belt, unlatching the clasp, and he removes his jeans and boxer briefs. Standing before me completely nude, he lets me take my fill of the view.

And a motherfucking incredible view it is. The man has muscles in places I didn't know one could have muscles. His thick cock is standing tall, a vein running along the length of it, and a drop of moisture glistens at the top. I whimper and squirm on the bed, eager for a taste of him.

A smile tugs at his mouth as his hand finds his cock. "You want to ride this again, peach?" he growls.

"Fuck yes," I say, confidence surging through me.

All of my manners have flown out the window, along with my sensibilities. He created this eager woman who doesn't hold back, and now he's going to have to deal with the consequences.

His hand stills as he watches me tug against my restraints. "I haven't shown you my favorite position yet. Though you with your ass turned up, riding against me, is a damn close second."

Wicked memories flash through my brain...my butt in the air, wantonly taking him from behind.

"You look good on all fours," he muses, remembering the same thing as me, it seems.

Nothing he says shocks me anymore. I've grown to love his filthy mouth, and my body lights up like a Christmas tree at his words. Despite my powerful release, I'm wet and hungry for more.

He unties my hands, carefully inspecting them before placing a tender kiss on the underside of each wrist. Then he slides a pillow underneath my ass, forcing my hips up off the bed several inches, and kneels between my parted legs, angling his cock toward me.

"Have you had a G-spot orgasm before, Brielle?"

A what? "No."

He lifts one of my legs over his shoulder and kisses my ankle. "Good. Another first I get to have." He positions the broad head of his cock against me and pushes forward, carefully at first, letting me adjust to him.

I open my mouth to ask him what's so special about the G-spot, when he begins moving his hips, pumping in and out in a steady rhythm, and my body clenches violently against him.

"Don't come yet, sweetheart." He chuckles. "Let me fuck you properly first."

With my ankle resting on his shoulder, he rocks back and forth, massaging that sensitive spot deep inside me, and soon I'm clawing at his back, begging him to let me come.

"Not yet, peach. I want you to feel everything I'm giving you." His dark, hungry eyes lock with mine and everything else fades into the night.

His sense of control is so straightforward and matter-of-fact that I can completely tune out the other noise in my brain, the many nonsensical things one thinks about on a daily basis. *Did I turn off the coffeemaker? I should go to the gym later. I need to return those pants that don't fit.*

Turning over all responsibility to this very capable man makes me feel *free*. All of my insecurities vanish. His touch forces me to stay in the moment and not let my distracted mind wander. He controls everything about my experience. His absolute dominance clears my brain of all the nonsense normally running rampant. It is bliss.

"Hale…" I cry, gripping his butt.

Forcing my hands to the bed, he holds me there. His teeth nip at the delicate skin on my ankle, and he sinks deeper inside me.

With every thrust, he claims his ownership over me. It's only supposed to be six weeks. So why does it feel like every kiss, every sweet, murmured word means more? Is he really going to let me walk away at the end of this?

"So fucking perfect..." He moans, his body shuddering as he tries to hold off his own orgasm. "Tightest pussy I've ever fucked."

Watching his expression change from dark seduction to one of complete surrender almost undoes me. Knowing I'm responsible for making this big, powerful man's body tremble and shake causes a rush of pride to rip through me.

When I work my hands free, so I can touch him, he doesn't stop me. He's just as consumed by our union as I am. Pressing my fingernails into his ass, I give in and my second orgasm of the night takes over, dragging me to that pleasurable place where nothing exists but his body buried within mine. A moment later, he lets go and marks me for the second time today.

With my heart pounding in my chest, I tug him down on top of me, holding him close, not caring about the warm, sticky mess between us. I feel his heart slamming against mine, and its bliss. This is what happiness feels like.

This moment is perfect, and I never want to let him go. A therapist would have a field day analyzing why I choose to spend my time with Hale rather than facing my future with Kirby.

Chapter Sixteen

HALE

A therapist would have a field day analyzing my work mentoring needy women. Yet tonight was something else entirely. What I just shared with Brielle is unlike anything I've done before. It wasn't just mentoring; it was more. I lose myself when I'm with her, and it fucking terrifies me.

I scrub my hands over my face, sitting up in bed. After we had sex, I fell asleep with Brielle draped across me. As I rise from the bed, awareness burns inside me that I've never fallen asleep at a client's house. Usually I can't get out of there fast enough, wanting a hot shower and the comfort of my own bed.

Yet right now, I can still smell Brielle's scent on my fingers, and I don't even want to wash my damn hands. She's marked me, and I know it isn't something I can simply wash away. My hands, hanging limp at my sides, already miss the feel of her, and my mouth yearns for the taste of her. My pulse pounds in my ears as I try to figure out what this all means.

She sits up, tugging the sheet to cover her breasts. "Are you leaving?"

I nod, forcing some composure in my voice. "Get some sleep. We'll talk soon."

She reaches a hand toward me. "Not yet. Stay...just a little longer."

For a moment I think she was going to ask me to stay the night, but we both know that can't happen.

I remain still, just standing there in her darkened bedroom, trying to figure out what the fuck I'm doing. I should just leave. Grab my pants, my wallet, my keys, and go home. But I don't. I release a heavy sigh, and when Brielle smiles and reaches out to me, I take her hand and let her pull me back into bed.

"What do you want?" I whisper.

"More."

"You sure about that?"

"Very," she says, her tone cheeky and her mouth tugged up in a smirk.

My hand slides between her legs, and her knees automatically fall open for me. She's learned to embrace her sexuality, and the knowledge that I've been the one to lead her there…it's very satisfying. But it's the look in her eyes that nearly undoes me. Complete trust. Trust I don't deserve, but she gives me—freely.

As my emotions roil inside me, I struggle to temper them. I can't show her everything right now; I don't want to. Instead I want to savor all of this, save some things that I can show her later so there will be new things to discover years from now. Where the fuck that thought came from, I don't know, but it's the honest-to-God truth.

We make love. Slowly. My mouth fuses to hers, capturing every breath, every moan while my body moves intimately above her.

When she whispers in the darkness and asks me what the lesson is, I quiet her with another kiss.

My silence is answer enough.

• • •

It's the middle of the night, dark and cool outside. When I finally get up to leave, Brielle doesn't even stir. I slide into my car and the engine roars to life.

The entire drive home, I can't stop the images of Brielle from playing through my mind. The way she looked spread open before me, the way her hot cunt squeezed me when she came. Goddamn, she's as close to perfect as you can get. Of course, she doesn't see that, which is why she hired me. Christ, I was hired to do a job, and my brain keeps fucking forgetting that. Because tonight? There was no lesson.

There was only my body joining with hers in a hungry rush of raw energy and emotion.

I tighten my grip on the wheel, completely beside myself. I never forget the lesson when I'm with a woman. *Never.* Everything I do—every touch, every caress, every command is meant to teach. But when I found Brielle in that club tonight, pressed up against some man who wasn't me, I lost it. I dragged her home like a fucking caveman and claimed her. It was only about her pleasure. All the wicked things I could show her body to prove to her that she was mine.

The sex isn't just good, it's mind blowing, earth shattering—for both of us. And I don't know how to handle that information. My world is quite literally rocked, thrown off its axis. A client has never gotten to me this way. I can barely maintain my composure and instruct her. She owns me.

And it's not only because she has the tightest pussy I've ever had. She affects me in ways I can't even explain. Her total submission to my every whim, her complete trust and faith in me, this process…it's staggering. Tonight I watched her chest rise and fall, felt the nervous energy zapping through her as she waited to see what I'd do next, which way I'd take her, knowing she'd allow it all. My cock hardens again just thinking about it.

The truth is I've started to notice little things about Brielle that I've never paid attention to before. Things that make her a real person and not a client, things that blur the lines of our arrangement. The way she leisurely stretches in bed after we're intimate, the way she tiptoes to the bathroom when she has to pee, the way her laughter lights up her entire face.

As a Dom, it's my responsibility to understand what my submissive needs. Brielle says she wants Kirby, but I know what she really needs is to be loved. To serve a man, and in turn feel that blissful pleasure that comes from a deep shared connection. Something so powerful, it's almost sacred. I can feel the underpinnings of that connection forming between us, and it scares the shit out of me. That wouldn't end well for either of us. I can't provide the things she desires. I've tried that route before and failed miserably.

Reece has warned me about getting emotionally attached to a submissive I'm training, and I'd always balked at him. It never seemed within the realm of possibility. Yet within a few short weeks, Brielle has brought me to the brink. My stomach churns when I realize what this means. I need to cancel the remainder of her sessions. The feeling is like a dumbbell sitting on my chest.

Walking into the dark apartment, I kick the door shut behind me, turning the dead bolt. I'm in for the night, as depressing as that sounds. My roommate isn't home, and I don't feel like being alone right now. I don't like the quiet stillness of the night; I still haven't gotten used to that. Nights are when I feel the most alone. And being alone stirs up memories I'd rather not think about. That's what my mentoring is supposed to be about—a different girl every week to keep my thoughts at bay, and occupy my time. Except there's only Brielle. Another thing I don't care to dwell on.

I glance around my room. A messy unmade bed, a fridge without food, though nothing appeals to me right now anyway. Maybe I should call Reece and go down to the club. Pay a visit to Chrissy. Yet that's not the answer either.

I'm edgy. And unsatisfied.

Frustrated, I grab a bottle of beer from the fridge and sink onto the couch, my mind once again on Brielle. Even that first night as my hand rested at her lower back, guiding her, I should have seen it. The clues that I was starting to feel territorial over her. My body knew before my mind.

Taking a long swallow of beer, I close my eyes and breathe. Even if I counted tonight with Brielle as a lesson—which we both know it wasn't—we're only at four sessions. How in the fuck could this woman all but destroy me in four meetings, I have no clue.

Changing my mind on the beer, I set it down and grab my phone to dial Reece. When he answers, there are voices and low music in the background.

"Cameron Hale, good to hear from you, brother."

"Hey, man. Anything going on tonight?" He knows me well. The tone of my voice and the fact that I'm calling at two a.m. are a good indication it's not such a good idea for me to be alone right now.

"There's always something going on," he says. "Why don't you come down?"

"Yeah, I'm thinking about it. Is Chrissy there?"

"She's here. Should I tell her to wait for you? She's looking to scene with somebody tonight."

"Yeah. I need to grab a shower, and I'll be right down."

Knowing Chrissy is waiting for me and my release is within sight, I hurriedly shower and dress. Then I'm back in my car, roaring down I-94 toward downtown Chicago and Crave within fifteen minutes.

• • •

When I think about releasing Brielle from her contract, I decide that tonight's performance is not how I want to end things. She came to me for a reason, and she's going to walk away from our deal with more confidence and skills than she ever had before.

One more lesson, that's the best I can offer. I just need to get my mind back in the right place. And there's nothing like a willing submissive ball-gagged and secured to a table to put your mind into focus.

Chrissy is wearing the signature black vintage lingerie that she prefers—silk stockings with seams running down the backs of her legs, a garter belt secured over her high-waisted black lace briefs, a push-up bra that conceals her chest, yet hints at her ample curves. Her lips are painted blood red, and they're currently open around a black rubber ball gag. She flinches at the blunt force of the riding crop as I lash it against the back of her thighs.

"Breathe through it," I encourage her, but my voice sounds weak, even to my ears.

Chrissy's eyes flash on mine. We haven't played together in weeks, not since I started seeing Brielle, and it feels strange, as if I'm rusty somehow.

She taps her fingers against the side of the table as I unbuckle the ball gag, removing it from her mouth.

"Sir?" she asks, blinking up at me.

"Yes?"

"Am I doing something wrong? Something you don't like? I can give you anything you allow tonight, sir." Her words are thick with suggestive undertones.

I've never fucked Chrissy, although I'm pretty sure Reece has. His brand of kink is more intense than mine, and based on the stories I've heard, often ends in hungry, crazed sex. I'm much more controlled in a scene. Or at least, I used to be. Tonight I'm just off, and I don't know why.

"You're doing fine. It's me, it's just—"

"The new girl you've been keeping busy with," she offers.

My gaze meets hers again. "Yes."

"Do you want to talk about it? It's almost morning. We could go get breakfast at that diner you like."

All of the adrenaline I've been running on for the last hour crashes, and I'm suddenly tired. And not at all into finishing the scene we've started. "Not tonight."

I release her from her binds and leave the room even more confused than when I arrived.

Chapter Seventeen

By Sunday, I've recovered from my night with Hale and am headed to Kirby's apartment. When I get there, he kisses me on the cheek and ushers me inside.

"I just need to catch the end of the game. You're cool hanging out for a little bit, right?" His eyes stray to the television without waiting for my response.

"Of course," I lie, even though I lined up an entire afternoon's worth of appointments and if we're late, it's going to throw off the entire day.

We sink down onto the couch and Kirby squeezes my thigh. "Glad you're here today. You've been busy lately."

"Yes," I say without expanding on what, or rather *who* was been keeping me occupied. I can never tell Kirby about Hale. He wouldn't understand.

When the game goes to commercial, Kirby heads into the kitchen and rummages around in the cabinets. "You want anything to eat? A beer?" he calls.

"No, I'm good," I call back as I take in the large apartment he shares with a roommate. It screams of bachelor pad. No personal touches, nothing to make it feel homey. I know his roommate is a lawyer at the firm where Kirby works, and that's about it.

Kirby returns with a beer and a bag of chips, which he happily crunches into as he drops down onto the couch beside me again. I can't help but notice the way he chews with his mouth open and wipes the crumbs from his fingers onto his pants.

"Is everything going okay with your roommate?"

"Yeah, why?" he asks.

"Because you want to move out."

He shrugs. "Nah, he's cool. Honestly, he's never home. I'm just ready to get my own place."

I nod, understanding that completely. After having roommates all through college, girls who were messy and "borrowed" my clothes without asking, I was more than ready for my own place.

"You've never even met him, have you?" he asks.

"Your roommate? Nope." Every time I've been here, his roommate is either gone or busy.

Kirby lifts his chin toward the hallway leading to the bedrooms. "Cameron, get your ass out here. I want you to meet someone," he shouts.

His plea is met with silence, and he shrugs.

"Is he even home?" I ask.

"Yeah. I heard him come in at like four in the morning, but he might still be sleeping."

"Don't you think it's strange I've never met your roommate?"

He shrugs again. "He's a mysterious guy. I don't know where he is half the time." Setting down the bag of chips, he wipes his hands and turns to face me.

"I never told you about why he moved in here with me, did I?"

I shake my head.

"It's some sad shit." His voice drops lower. "His parents died his senior year of high school, and he was a mess, naturally. He went away to college, and freshman year, he met this girl named Tara. She filled him with hope and love, and all that shit people look for. They dated all through college, all through law school. She was his rock."

Kirby picks up his beer and takes a long swallow before continuing. "I actually met her once at a firm holiday party, his first year at the law firm. She was quiet and kind of withdrawn, if you asked me, but to him, God, you could see the love he had for her radiating from his eyes. She was all he had. His everything. He proposed with a huge diamond that he'd saved up for all year. I swear, his entire first-year earnings went toward that ring. While all the other first-years were trying to claw our way out from under a mountain of student loan debt, Cameron was scraping and saving for her."

"What happened?" My hands are curled around a throw pillow. I clutch it to my chest, anticipating the worst, that she was somehow taken from him too soon.

"He left work early one day—he'd won a massive case, actually the one that got him promoted from junior associate to associate, and wanted to celebrate. When he got to their apartment, she was on her hands and knees, taking it up the ass by one of his best friends."

My hand flies to my mouth. "That's horrible."

He nods. "Fucking tragic. She was everything to him. After that, you could see the light in his eyes dimmed. He lost faith in everything that day. Lost the last little piece of him. He fucking moped around for months. He moved in here with only a duffel bag and a whole bunch of suits. It's been two years, and he's finally getting back to himself."

"That's so sad," I murmur, completely absorbed in his story. My heart hurts for Kirby's roommate, and I realize his situation is even harder than my own of wanting someone you can't have.

"I know. Every time I think about wanting a relationship, I remember the months he spent broken and sulking, and I decide that putting that much trust in another person is just not something I want to do."

"Are you sure it's a good idea to move out, Kirby? You've painted this picture that he has no one left in his life."

He chuckles. "Trust me, he'll be fine. I'm pretty sure he's been out nailing a different girl every night to make up for that bitch whore of a fiancée."

Okay then.

"We better get going," I say, glancing at the time on my phone. "I don't want us to be late for all the appointments I've set."

"A few more minutes, ladybug." He squeezes my knee, eyes on the TV again.

As I observe Kirby watching his game, I'm having a hard time remembering what I ever saw in him. He picks at his teeth, chews with his mouth open, ignores a phone call from his mom, and shouts at the TV. And worst of all is that he hardly notices me.

The longer I sit here, the more I realize that I'm better than that. I don't want a man I have to convince. I want someone who wants me for *me*. My mind wanders to Hale. He always makes me feel desired. A smile tugs at my lips as I stare blankly at the TV and wonder where he is and what he's doing today.

My cell phone chimes from my purse and I fish it out, wondering who's texting me. It's probably Julie.

When I see that it's Hale, my heart riots in my chest, knowing he was thinking of me at the exact same moment I was thinking of him.

HALE: What are you doing?

I smile as I type out my reply.

BRIELLE: Hanging out with Kirby.

Once I've typed that, cold dread washes over me. What if he challenges me to do something bold…like seduce Kirby?

HALE: Is he every bit as dreamy as you recalled?

BRIELLE: Of course.

The words feel fake, but it's what I'm supposed to say. The whole reason Hale is helping me is because of my interest in Kirby. Just then, angry music blares loudly from down the hall, or more specifically, from his roommate's bedroom.

I steal a glance at Kirby, my eardrums protesting the obtrusive noise. "Does he have a heavy-metal obsession?"

He shrugs. "Not normally."

I look back down at my phone to see a new message from Hale.

HALE: Tonight. You're mine.

My belly tightens with nervous anticipation.

When we started our working relationship, I was under the impression that we'd meet once weekly for six weeks. We just saw each other last night, but he wasn't about to get an argument from me. Things have begun to feel more domestic between us.

Hale isn't my boyfriend, but hell if my brain knows that. The intimacy we shared last night, God, I can't even think about it without my face getting hot. And I'm pretty certain that second time last night, when I reached for his hand and urged him back to bed, wasn't part of any lesson. It was just two lost souls searching for comfort together.

I text him back, already feeling the steady thrum of my heart picking up speed.

BRIELLE: When and where?

HALE: You'll see.

His reply is coy and guarded, but before I can ask what he means, Kirby rises from the couch and clicks off the TV. "You ready?"

"Sure." I stuff my phone back into my purse, already hot with anticipation for tonight.

• • •

After several hours of touring condos in high-rise buildings around the city, I finally make my way home. There's a large black box with a red ribbon waiting for me outside my door. Somehow I know it's from Hale. I take it inside, eager to see what it holds.

I head into my bedroom and set the box down on my bed. It's fairly weighty, and I have no clue what it could be. Lifting the lid, I see crisp white paper lining the inside and a square card nestled on the top. I pull the card from its envelope, appreciating how thick the card stock feels between my fingers.

The message is brief, handwritten in neat black ink.

Be at the corner of Lakeshore Drive and Grand Avenue. 7 p.m.

—H

Peeling back the tissue paper, I discover the contents of the mysterious box. A white lacy G-string and matching demi-cup bra, along with a thick knee-length wool coat in the most bright, vibrant shade of red. The coat is gorgeous. Somehow I know I'm meant to be wearing nothing but this coat and these underthings when I meet him tonight. The idea sends a small thrill racing through me. I set everything down on my bed and then head to shower.

As I get ready, my phone buzzes constantly with sweet little texts from him. One to confirm I got the package, another telling me he's excited for tonight, and a third that says he can't wait to see me. I've never had a man make me feel this special before, or put so much thought into a date.

By the time I'm slipping on my coat over my new bra and panty set, I feel desirable and ready for some naughty fun.

Chapter Eighteen

HALE

This is it. My last lesson with Brielle. All morning, I fought for perspective and failed. After tonight's festivities, I'm going to tell her that she's ready. That she's learned all I can teach her.

I don't know how she'll take the news. Me? I'm so confused and frustrated that I feel like fucking punching something at the thought of not seeing her again after this.

I'm dressed in a suit and tie, and told her to be waiting at the corner of Lakeshore and Grand. I glance at my watch and see that I'm right on time. Watching from the dark-tinted window of the limousine, I spot her. She glances around and then checks her phone. She's wearing the red wool coat belted snugly and holds a small jeweled clutch. The Chicago winter makes it necessary, but I can't wait to peel the coat from her body and see what's underneath it. See if she knew to follow my subtle instruction.

At my direction, the driver pulls to a stop at the corner beside her, and Brielle's eyes light up. I step out and greet her, pulling her body to mine and kissing her deeply. She doesn't hesitate; her mouth opens against me, her tongue making little circles with mine. It's fucking heaven. She smells lightly of perfume and soap, and her hair is down, in long curls that flutter in the wind.

"Let's get you warmed up," I whisper near her ear.

She nods and lets me take her hand to help her into the waiting limo, which is white as I requested. I may not be a noble knight on a white horse, but she deserves one, and this is the best I can do.

"Wow. A limo? What's on the agenda tonight?" Her eyes sparkle as she takes it all in, sliding across the leather seat with a happy smile. And suddenly all the trouble I've gone through planning tonight is immediately worth it.

"You'll see," I say.

She doesn't know it yet, but I'm going to push her further than I ever have before. My cock twitches at the thought. I will prove to us both that this isn't some fucking fairy tale. I have needs she can't possibly satisfy, and she deserves a tenderness that I can't possibly provide.

Everything will be settled after tonight. And I will send her off, ready to use all her techniques to win over the one she wants, the man who is a safe choice for her.

Plucking the waiting bottle of champagne from its bucket of ice, I free the cork. Brielle smiles at the popping sound. I pour us each a glass in the tall flutes, and we clink glasses.

"Cheers. To Kirby," I say coolly.

Her face falls, her eyebrows pinching together. "I thought you said no names."

"Seems kind of pointless when I already know it, doesn't it, Brielle?"

She chews on her lower lip and shrugs. "I guess so."

"To Kirby," I repeat, bringing my glass to hers again. "One lucky son of a bitch."

This gets a smile from her, and we both sip our champagne.

"So your time with him went well today?" I ask, trying to temper my curiosity.

Her gaze wanders out the window, and she takes another drink before answering. "Of course."

As we sip our champagne in silence, I wish I could pick up on what she's thinking. I need to hold it together. I can sense myself slipping, and Brielle is watching me with a curious stare.

Fucking hell.

When did my life get so goddamned complicated? This whole venture was supposed to be about easy fun, exploring women's sexual fantasies, and a release for my dominant side. Instead it's become a game I don't think I can win. One that's going to leave me old and alone with nothing to show for my efforts, just like Nana fears.

I tip back my head, downing the rest of my champagne, and set down my glass. It's game time.

• • •

When we arrive at the hotel suite I've booked for the night, Brielle walks from room to room, checking out the place. It's opulent, almost too much for our uses tonight. I plan on fucking her as many times and in as many places as possible, and still, I know we won't even make it into half the rooms.

When she returns to the living room, where I'm waiting for her beside a cart of drinks, I smile warmly at her. "Take off your coat. Stay a while."

Her answering smile lights up her face. "You'd like that, wouldn't you, sir?"

"Fuck yes, I would."

She slowly releases the belt, letting me catch a glimpse of the dip in her smooth belly, the white lace at the top of her panties.

My erection presses awkwardly against the front of my slacks. But fuck it, she knows what she does to me by now. No need to fake a sense of control I don't possess.

I wait for her to drop the coat from her shoulders, but she stops, her eyes lifting to mine. "Are we going out? Or what's the plan?"

I force a breath into my lungs, trying to get myself to calm the fuck down. We have all night. No need to pounce on her like the tasty treat she is within two minutes of entering the hotel suite. "We're staying here tonight."

"All night?" she asks, her nose scrunching up in a way that looks damn cute on her.

We both know that's a huge fucking step. We've never spent the night together. "Yes. Is that okay, Brielle?"

Her gaze slips away from mine, noting the cart of drinks with various bottles and mixers along with a bucket of ice, over to the dining table where fussy finger foods and hors d'oeuvres and desserts are artfully arranged, and then back to the hallway that leads to the master bedroom. Her smile falters, the corners of her mouth twitching.

This is too real, too intimate, and she knows it. Her questioning blue eyes see everything. All my motivations are stripped bare; I don't need to say a word. She was expecting something crazy, but all she's getting is me. I want to pretend she's mine for one last night before I have to release her.

I cross the room and stand directly in front of her, pushing my hand inside her coat to place it firmly on her waist and drag her close.

"It's just us tonight," I whisper, fighting the urge to kiss her mouth.

"Where are the ropes? The whips? The chains?"

"You want ropes?" I ask, my tone hollow. Maybe I can't give her what she needs after all.

"I don't understand," she says softly.

"BDSM isn't always about the ropes and implements, Brielle. Sure, I like the toys in my bag, and I like them even better when I'm using them to tease and pleasure you, but at the very core of it, it's about the connection between two people."

She nods slightly. My words make sense, at the surface, at least. But why we're here, sharing an encounter that will deepen *our* connection when she's not even mine...yeah, that's the million-dollar question.

I've never in my life spent money like this on a date with a client. One hundred dollars for the lingerie, six hundred for the coat that fits her beautifully and brings out the rose color in her cheeks, a couple hundred for the limo, and a thousand dollars for the posh hotel suite. She's worth all this and more.

The money doesn't matter. I simply wanted our last night together to be perfect, one that I could remember for years to come. Because something tells me that my head and my heart won't be the same after this.

"Would you like a drink? Something to eat?" I ask, my voice low. All I want is her, but I suppose I should be polite and tend to her needs first.

She nods. "Yes, thank you."

Slipping my hand from her waist, I belt her jacket again, realizing she'll probably get cold wearing nothing but the tiny panties and bra.

"Come sit. I'm going to serve you tonight."

Her eyes flash on mine while her mouth curves into a surprised smirk. "What's gotten into you?"

I shrug. The truth is, I wish I fucking knew. "A real man takes care of his lady's needs before his own. Don't forget, everything is a lesson. Once I turn you loose back into the dating world, I want you to remember all of this, and not to settle for something less than you deserve."

She nods, then takes a seat in one of the oversized upholstered chairs at the edge of the dining room, slipping off her heels and curling her legs under her.

"Besides, my mother always used to say 'manners make the man.'"

"That's nice," she says.

"The fifteen-year-old me didn't think so. I didn't see why manners were something I had to think about when my friends didn't care, and the girls in school seemed to go for the guys who treated them like they were disposable."

Brielle's quiet, but I can tell she's hanging on my every word. I rarely talk about my past, and I've never shared with her something about my mother.

"When I questioned her, my mother told me that acting like a gentleman would make smart, beautiful women notice me and important men want to give me a job."

"And was she right?" Brielle asks, a smile creeping into her voice.

"I should say so." I toss a wink at her over my shoulder.

I can't resist mixing her the same cocktail she ordered that first night. The timid set of her shoulders and flushed cheeks had my cock hardening even then. She sat at the bar alone, quietly sipping this very drink as she waited for me to change her entire world.

I'm playing nice right now, but the sinking feeling in my gut reminds me that tonight is a one-time deal. I'm supposed to be showing her every wicked thing in my playbook, reaffirming her decision that the man she really wants isn't me. We'll see if I can pull that off. Because, hell, I'm fucking terrified I'd change my entire life if she asked me to.

Focusing on my game face, I hand her a crystal tumbler filled with peach liqueur, ice, and fizzy club soda. She brings her lips to the glass and smiles when she tastes it.

"You remembered."

"Of course. It's my job to remember my clients' likes and dislikes."

Her smile fades at the word *client*. I sense we both know that she's so much more to me. All the effort I've put into tonight should prove that.

After we've polished off our second round of drinks and our plates are empty, the mood grows heavy around us.

Brielle's gaze floats over to where my black bag is still sitting beside the door.

I raise one eyebrow at the slow smile that blooms on her lips. "You seem eager."

"You said no ropes, whips, or chains, so why should I be anything other than excited?"

"Just because I'm not going to tie you up and flog you tonight doesn't mean you won't be at my mercy."

My tongue slipped and said *tonight*, but what I really meant was *ever*. This is it, and I need to remember that.

Brielle looks contemplative, and I wonder when she's going to grace me with the thoughts lurking in her mind. It only takes a few more sips from her cocktail. "What's the end game here?"

"The end game?" Hell, now I'm really curious.

She swirls the drink in her glass. "I'm just curious. It's obvious you have a well-paying job. You wear suits to work and can afford places like this," she gestures to the posh hotel suite, "and I know you're not looking to find a companion. So why do it?"

"We covered this before, Brielle. I like instructing. I like taking a woman where she's never dared to go before. I like being the one to open her eyes to something more."

She chews on her lip, unsatisfied with my response. "Do you think you'll ever give it up?"

Her questions have gotten too personal. I could put a stop to this right now with one barked command, but I won't. She wants to poke around in my head, but I doubt she'll like what she finds. "Not planning on it."

"So even if you found the perfect sub, someone you were compatible with inside and outside the bedroom, you wouldn't stop seeing clients?"

That would take a huge leap of faith on my part, and trust is something I have a hard time with, given my past. The wounds are still fresh. Raw. I can't bare myself that completely with her, not while she's still hung up on Kirby.

Rising to my feet, I head to the door to retrieve the bag. "Go into the bedroom, take off your coat, and wait for me."

Wordlessly, she obeys, her soft footfalls on the carpet fading down the hall.

I grab a few ice cubes from the bar before heading that way myself. When I step into the bedroom, she's standing near the dresser in the large room, running her fingers along the crystal vase that rests there. The curve of her ass in the G-string has my cock swelling.

I stand behind her and lower my mouth to her ear. "Turn around and let me see you."

She turns slowly, letting me appreciate the full effect of her curves filling out the delicate lingerie.

Jesus. Fuck. I slip one of the ice cubes into her mouth. "Suck."

Her eyes widen and zero in on mine. I love it how my simplest command surprises her. Her lips close around the ice, and her eyes flutter closed. With the other ice cube, I circle her belly button, and her stomach jumps in surprise.

"You're mine tonight. My plaything. To do with what I wish. Do you understand?"

She nods slowly.

"Answer me, pet."

"Yes, sir."

Her skin breaks out in chill bumps as I move the ice over to her hip bone, down toward her panties. She sucks in a breath and holds it. I drop to my knees, my mouth following the path of dissolving ice, my tongue licking away the sting of cold.

I tease her with my mouth over the front of her panties until she's writhing to get closer. It's not clear which of us I'm teasing, though, because I want nothing more than to taste her sweet pussy.

We're still standing in front of the mirror, and I turn her to face it. Her chest is flushed, and her eyes are clouded with arousal. If tonight is really meant to be our last lesson, the sentimental side of me that so rarely comes out needs to make sure she's ready.

"I want you to look at yourself and tell me what you see," I whisper near her ear, letting my lips brush her skin.

She fidgets, placing her hands over her belly as if inspecting herself in the mirror is too invasive despite all the things we've shared.

After a moment, her eyes lift to mine and she smiles. "I see a handsome man who makes me feel desirable."

Shaking my head, I correct her. "No, tell me what you see when you look at you."

A quiet stillness settles around us as she studies herself in the mirror. Her hair is long and glossy, her breasts are small but pert, and the juncture between her thighs is covered in white lace, but my hope is that she knows her worth beyond those physical traits.

"I don't know how to do this. I'm sorry." With a defeated tone, she dips her head, tucking her chin toward her chest.

Fuck. I didn't mean to make her feel awkward and self-conscious. But women don't come with a manual, and so sometimes even I stumble.

"Can I tell you what I see?"

Meeting my reflection in the mirror, she nods.

"I see a beautiful, smart woman who had the courage to pursue her goals, who has shown strength in each act of submission." My knuckles trace her sides, ghosting over her ribs. "I see someone fierce and loyal and brave. Someone who is willing to sacrifice her comfort zone in the search for love. Someone who's giving and kind in the bedroom." My lips linger at the side of her neck. "You're perfection, peach." In every way.

Tears glitter in her eyes, and she chews on her lip as she blinks them away. I'm not sure why, but I wanted her to know how I feel about her. Even if I could take it back, I wouldn't.

Needing to change the mood, I release her. "Lie down on the bed."

She nods and quickly heads to the large bed, depositing herself on one side of it.

I remove the candle from inside my bag and light it on the dresser. It casts a subtle glow into the room, giving everything a dreamy, romantic feel. The rich, warm fragrance fills the air. This candle, which was meant to set the scene and relax her, has become so much more. It's now a scent I'll always associate just with Brielle.

Slowly and methodically, I remove her bra and panties. I gaze down at her, wanting to commit to memory her flawless skin, the rise and fall of her chest, the way her nipples pebble in anticipation of my mouth.

Her eyes are on mine. "How do you want me?"

I shake my head. "Just like this." I pull my shirt off over my head and let my pants and boxers fall to the floor before joining her on the bed again. Moving my body over hers, I kiss her deeply, savoring each lick of her tongue like I'm a dying man enjoying his last meal.

When she reaches down and takes me in her hand, I don't stop her. Her fist curls around me, and I grunt.

"Inside me, please," she breathes against my mouth.

When I reach between us and feel that she's soaked, I align myself with her. "Be still, okay?"

She nods her consent.

I lift her legs so her pelvis is tilted up and place her ankles on my shoulders. "I want you to feel me tomorrow."

Brielle, ever trusting, blinks up at me.

"Eyes down here, pretty girl. Watch." With my thumb, I part her folds and push the head of my cock just inside. Her pussy is squeezing me already, and I harden even more. I make sure her eyes are still on the action and when I see that they are, I push forward again. Two more inches of me slip inside. *Fuck.*

She whimpers, her voice throaty and full of need. "More, Hale. Harder," she begs.

She wants me to slam home and fuck her until she comes. But tonight is about control.

"Patience," I growl, pushing inside her warmth until I'm halfway buried.

Sharp fingernails dig into my ass cheeks, and she throws her head back against the pillow.

"Eyes, sweetheart," I remind her. "Keep them on my cock. I want you to watch how I fuck you." The truth is I want to ruin her for all other men. I want her to understand my cock is the only one that can make her feel this way.

She opens her eyes and her gaze drifts from mine, down my chest and abs to settle on my throbbing erection. *Good girl.*

Thrusting forward, I move slowly, allowing her body to stretch to accommodate me. I give her every last inch of me, and once I'm buried within the snug heat of her, I hiss out a breath.

We move together, our bodies growing slick with sweat, my hands digging into her hips as I pull her closer. Her inner muscles tighten and tremble, and I lean down near her ear, encouraging her to let go, slowing my movements to let her ride out the wave of pleasure her orgasm provides.

I can't hold back any longer. I thrust hard, overcome with pleasure at the way her tight body squeezes mine. My release hits me hard and fast, obliterating all my control. I tug Brielle close, holding her tightly as our heartbeats slam together.

Eventually, I rise from the bed, my body missing her warmth beside me. I go to the bathroom to get her a warm cloth, and when I return, I find her curled up in the center of the bed, her cheeks damp with tears.

"Brielle?" My chest tightens and a feeling of dread washes over me. I join her on the bed and lift her onto my lap. "Tell me why you're crying," I whisper near her temple. I want to soothe her fears, make everything better, but I know I can't.

"This was never supposed to happen," she sobs. "You warned me, but it's just so overwhelming."

I pull her close, planting a kiss on her forehead. "I know, pet, I know. It will pass. I told you, it's just the rush of endorphins wreaking havoc on your system." I hate myself for saying these words. I'm falling in love with her, and I want all of these emotions overwhelming her to be just for me. But she nods, accepting my explanation.

I hold her while she cries and finally, once she's quiet, we lay in the huge hotel bed, curled together as we watch an old black-and-white movie.

"Are you going to see Kirby tomorrow?" I whisper. I'm not sure why, but the curiosity is killing me.

"No. I'm working tomorrow."

I nod, feeling relief and shame mix together. Even if she's not seeing him tomorrow, I know that soon she's going to win him over, and it's a deeply disturbing thought.

Our last night together feels heavy with meaning. If these are the last of my minutes with her, I'm happy to spend them listening to her sleepy sounds and enjoying the warmth of her body curled against mine.

• • •

In the morning, my sense of purpose is renewed. I dress while Brielle is still asleep and slip out of the hotel room. It's better than having to hear her say good-bye. Last night I took things that weren't mine to take, we grew closer than we should have, and I don't want to see the look of regret that's probably in her eyes this morning. Brielle and I are two different people. I no longer possess that same hopeful optimism that love conquers all.

When I met Tara, she become my entire world. I fell hard and fast, and never doubted for a second that she'd be at my side when we were both old and gray. And for years, things were great.

Wanting to make her my wife, I bought her the best ring money could buy. She deserved it after watching me scrape my way through law school, and living in cheap student housing with me. As we lay curled together at night on our lumpy mattress, I used to whisper to her how I'd give her the world if I could. All my love, promises, and sacrifice weren't enough for her, though, because one day I came home early and found her fucking my best friend, Troy. He was a good friend, and while it hurt to know he betrayed me, it was her unfaithfulness that destroyed me. I'd been ready to devote my life to her.

After that, Reece proved what a good friend he is by cutting Troy from his life completely. He felt the betrayal almost as deeply as I did. That's when I began exploring the BDSM lifestyle Reece is so fond of, and felt immediately at home. Control. Discipline. Never getting too close. It was the only type of relationship I saw myself having with a woman. The exchange of power was exactly what I craved.

After Tara left me for another man, I became the other man so I never had to feel that kind of hurt again, so that I could never be left again. I don't involve my heart, and I won't ever give myself away completely in these interactions. That's why I never tell them my name. Because I won't exist when we're done.

It's this mindset that I try to summon as I head off to meet with Chrissy. I push the thoughts of Brielle that plague me as far away as possible. Today is about Chrissy and the future she's always dreamed of.

On my way out to the suburbs, I sent a text to Brielle.

HALE: Peach, something has come up. I'm sorry for the change in plans, but last night's session will be our last.

Her response is simple.

BRIELLE: Okay.

I'm not sure what I was expecting. An argument? Her demanding an explanation? Suddenly I wish I had told her in person so I could see her face, watch her expression change. Would it be relief, indifference, or disappointment I saw reflected in her pretty features? Not knowing is driving me insane.

When I arrive at the address Chrissy sent me, I step out of the car to greet her. She's standing in the driveway, surveying her surroundings. When she spins to face me, I hiss out a breath. *Holy shit.*

"Chrissy?" I reach for her. "What the fuck happened?" Lifting her chin with two fingers, I force her eyes to meet mine.

She squeezes her eyes closed and whimpers.

There are fingertip bruises around her throat and a dark mark under one eye that her makeup doesn't cover. Her lower lip is swollen and red with bite marks.

"Chrissy? Answer me."

"Don't," she pleads with me. She knows I won't let this drop until the motherfucker who got rough with her pays for his harsh treatment.

I press closer, my thumbs stroking her cheeks as I hold her face near mine. "Goddamn it. Who did this?"

She shakes her head. "It was nothing I didn't ask for. Come on, the real estate agent's here. Let's go inside."

Her words send me into a frenzy. She asked for this shit?

"Please, Hale," she begs.

Fuck.

Today is supposed to be a happy day, so I take Chrissy's hand and turn toward the little bungalow I'm helping her buy, but a loud gasp startles us both.

Brielle.

She's standing several feet away, watching me interact with Chrissy. Wearing her red coat, she looks so beautiful and fragile, I want to weep. Her eyes have welled with tears, which she works to blink away.

I want to go to her, want to tell her it's not what it looks like, but the cliché of a lie dies on my lips.

Brielle's watchful eyes don't miss a thing. Not the bruises decorating Chrissy's neck, or the way she has a death grip on my hand. Deep hurt and betrayal is written all over Brielle's face.

Sensing the tense standoff happening between me and Brielle, Chrissy shifts beside me. "Is everything okay?"

"Fine," I lie.

Brielle sucks in a deep breath and straightens her shoulders. I know she's hurt, but pretending she's okay. She's pretending we didn't just fuck each other's brains out last night, that we don't have a connection neither of us can explain.

"Are you guys ready to see the house? I think you're going to love it," she manages, her voice lifting with a slight tremor.

Goddamn it.

I'm itching to take her into my arms and hold her, quiet all her fears, tell her everything, expose myself, and beg for her forgiveness. Instead I merely stand here. I'm not about to expose Brielle as one of my clients. We both signed that nondisclosure agreement, and I took that seriously. It could affect her professional reputation if word got out; not that Chrissy would say anything, but still, I wouldn't put her at risk.

It takes Brielle several tries to get the lockbox open, her hands are shaking that badly.

When I reach for her, she tugs her hand away as if I'm poison. Maybe I am.

"I've got it," she barks, then realizes her mistake and puts on a smile for Chrissy. "See? We're in." She pushes open the front door and motions us inside out of the cold.

The house is a two-bedroom, two-bath fifties-style bungalow, as is common in this area. The hardwood floors creak when we walk from room to room, exploring. The bathrooms need updating, but the kitchen was recently renovated, and the walls and carpets are all fresh and neutral.

Chrissy has done a good job. She's been saving for three years to buy a place of her own, move out of that rundown shoebox she calls an apartment. When I told her I'd help her with the down payment, it sped up her timeline significantly.

Chrissy stops to face me in the living room, where a quaint stone fireplace sits under a rustic wood mantel. Brielle is never out of sight, and I can feel her presence as if she's cast a shadow over me.

"What do you think?" Chrissy asks.

"I think it's great. More important, what do you think?" She'll be the one with her name on the thirty-year mortgage, not me.

"I love it. I feel like it's already home. Fires burning right there," she points to the fireplace, "and a little garden in the backyard…" Her voice trails off and her eyes glisten.

"Merry Christmas," I whisper to her, and she wraps her arms around me, squeezing my waist.

She looks into my eyes and wipes at her own. "You're amazing, you know that?"

I force a smile, painfully aware that Brielle is watching this entire exchange.

Before I can process what's happened, I'm standing outside on the sidewalk, watching Brielle get into her car and speed away.

Goddamn it. I've never felt so out of control.

It's time to start taking on clients again. Stop this bullshit fantasy from playing out any further.

Chapter Nineteen

BRIELLE

My vision blurs as I sob big, ugly tears the entire drive home. I make it there in record time and tear through my apartment. The first thing I do is strip off my new red coat and stuff it in the trash can.

Something's come up, his text said. Hell yeah, something came up! He's apparently buying a house with a woman—a woman who looks like she's been used as a punching bag, which I can only assume was during a session of rough sex.

I'm not even angry; I'm broken. Destroyed. A man I had fallen head over heels for is not who I thought he was. It was all some game. I paid him handsomely for his services, and that was all it was to him. A down payment on his future with another woman. The painful realization that I meant nothing to him slams into me, and I feel weak.

Grabbing my laptop, I delete my profile from the dating site, delete every stupid message I saved. I delete his texts, and then his number from my phone. It's as though he never even existed. If only my aching heart could mirror that feeling.

I sink onto the couch and let the tears flow. I consider calling Julie, but the idea of admitting how foolish I've been doesn't appeal to me. Of course I knew better than to fall for him, yet I did it anyway. I gave myself to him completely, in every sense of the word, but it was all for nothing. Now he's done with me, and I feel lost. I don't know what comes next.

As painful as it is, I can't stop the memory of seeing him with that bruised and battered woman from replaying in my brain. I recall the careful way he was with her, the way his hand danced at her lower back, and she gazed up adoringly into his eyes as they spoke in hushed voices.

Not only did he lie about having a girlfriend, but he's not at all who I thought he was. He's violent. Brutal. Not at all the man I dreamed him to be.

Several hours later, I've had two glasses of wine and am soaking in a hot bath when my phone rings.

It's Kirby.

I consider letting it go to voice mail; I don't want to talk to anyone right now. But then I remember what this entire experiment was about. Taking charge of my future.

Mustering some enthusiasm, I answer. "Hi there," I say, forcing a neutral tone.

"Hey, ladybug. I need a favor."

"I'm listening…"

Chapter Twenty

I'm arriving home from the gym when Kirby corners me in the kitchen. I've been hitting the gym hard lately in an effort to move on, but all it's done is frustrate me.

"You're going to the company Christmas party tonight, right?" he asks, shoving a bottle of water at me.

Christ, I forgot all about that with everything that's happened in the last few days. "Of course. You bringing anyone?"

Kirby shrugs. "Yeah, I called my fuck buddy, asked her to meet me there."

I nod. "Cool. I'll probably just go solo."

The fact that Kirby's been sleeping with someone is news to me. He must go to her place, because for at least the past several months, he hasn't brought anyone home.

I shower and dress in a tuxedo, as the invitation said black tie required. Just what I want to do on my Saturday, after wearing a suit to work all week. When I'm ready, I find Kirby dressed similarly and standing in the kitchen, opening a bottle of Scotch. There are two glasses on the counter before him.

"Toast before we go?" he asks.

"Why not." I accept the glass of amber liquor and clink the edge to his.

"To a better fucking year next year," he says, smiling as if he's got me all figured out.

I make an affirmative noise in my throat and down the liquid, appreciating the smoky flavor that greets my tongue. "Did you like any of the places Brielle showed you?"

His surprised gaze lands on mine. "I didn't know you knew my real estate agent was Brielle."

Fuck. I shrug. "Yeah, you mentioned it in passing."

He shakes his head like he doesn't recall it, but isn't going to argue. "Yeah. There's a townhome I want to put an offer on. I'm going to ask Brielle if she'll forgo her commission on the sale, you know, as a favor, so I can afford a little more."

My eyebrows knit together. Hasn't he fucked her over enough? She's wasted five years of her life pining after him, and now he's going to fuck her out of the several thousand dollars she'd make for doing her job. *Fucking asshole.* He's not good enough for her. A fact I've always known, but is clearer now than ever.

Kirby glances at the clock on the stove. "We should get going."

"Sure."

We head outside and stand at the corner, waiting for a taxi to stop.

"Oh, my date canceled at the last minute, but I called Brielle. I knew she wouldn't have anything going on tonight. It looks like you'll finally get to meet her."

My mouth goes dry and the shot of alcohol churns in my stomach. I consider making up an excuse and heading back alone to the apartment, but decide, fuck it. Let her see me for what I really am.

It's go time.

Chapter Twenty-One

BRIELLE

I have no idea why I agreed to this.

I gaze longingly out of the window of the cab, watching as couples outfitted in long evening gowns and tuxedoes make their way inside the historic hotel.

"Lady? You getting out?"

I glance at the cab driver and sigh. "Yes. Sorry. Here, keep the change." I hand him a twenty and open the door to the frigid air.

A cold wind lifts my hair as I shuffle inside the revolving doors as quickly as I can in my black gown and heels, and grab my phone from my wristlet. I expected to see a text from Kirby, but there's nothing.

With a sigh, I decide to head into the ballroom to see if I can locate him. Or a bar. A drink sounds fabulous right now.

I agreed to be his date tonight, not because I was delusional enough to think this was an actual date—it was his work party—but because my goal all along has been to see if there's the possibility of a spark between us. I couldn't say no, despite how badly I wanted to hide in my apartment and sulk for at least another week.

An attendant by the double doors asks for my name and I give it, adding that I'm meeting Kirby Norton here.

He nods. "He's right over there." He points to the bar, and my nerves calm when I spot Kirby. He's leaning against the bar with a bottle of beer in his hand, laughing at something the man next to him is saying.

I cross the room, heading right toward him. I'm not in the mood to make small talk, or laugh politely at jokes right now. In fact, maybe I can talk Kirby into leaving early and taking me to that Thai place I like.

Kirby watches me approach. "Ladybug," he says and grabs me in a hug. "You look...beautiful tonight," he says.

"Thank you," I murmur.

I made an effort. After spending the last several days in yoga pants with tear marks streaking my face, tonight I pampered myself with a long soak, thorough makeup application, and am wearing a strapless floor-length black gown with jewels at my throat.

He introduces me to the man next to him. "Brielle, this is my boss, Mr. Goldstein. Brielle is an old friend."

I shake the man's hand, my mind turning over the way he said *old friend.*

"Let me get you something to drink," Kirby offers. "What's that plum thingy you like?"

"It's peach, not plum." My face heats with the secret knowledge that my affinity for peach liqueur inspired my safe word.

"Right," he says, signaling the bartender.

Mr. Goldstein leans down to whisper, "It's an open bar. I hope you're not falling for his act."

I chuckle, assuring him that I'm well aware of Kirby's cheapness.

Once we have our drinks, I let Kirby lead me away and introduce me to various men and women that he works with. My ability to make small talk is nonexistent. I find myself barely able to nod and manage one-word responses. The old me would have been handing out business cards and using the evening as a networking tool. I'm just not in the mood to socialize, and I'm starting to think it was a terrible idea to come out tonight.

I tug Kirby aside on his third trip to the bar. "I'm sorry, but I'm going to cut out early."

"Really? Already?"

I nod. "Yeah, I'm sorry. I'm just not in the mood to meet a bunch of new people tonight."

He nods, seeming to understand. "Okay. I'll call you a cab."

"Thank you." I'm glad he's not going to try to talk me into staying.

"There's just one more person I want you to meet."

I'm about to refuse when my eyes lock with Hale's. His dark eyes are pinned on mine. Shivers race across my body.

Holy fuck! How did he know I was here?

Kirby places a possessive hand on my shoulder. "Brielle, this is my roommate, Cameron."

My entire world drops out from beneath me.

Hale—or Cameron, or whoever he is—strides right up to me as if he owns me. He looks devastatingly handsome in his expensive black tuxedo, crisp white shirt, and perfectly styled black silk bowtie. A tie, that if I know him at all, will likely be used later to bind the hands of some poor girl.

My knees feel weak, and the liqueur I consumed churns violently in my belly.

"Peach." He lifts my hand to his mouth and kisses the back of it. When his full, warm lips touch my skin, my body revolts and I draw my hand back.

"Don't," I warn him, my tone venomous.

"Do you two know each other?" Kirby asks, his confusion palpable.

"Quite well. Isn't that right, Brielle?"

Hale is drunk. I've never seen him drink before, but his dilated pupils and the slight drawl to his voice is a dead giveaway.

"Don't tell me she's one of the mystery girls you've been fucking." The shock painted across Kirby's normally relaxed face is almost painful. I actually feel bad for him.

Hale doesn't deny it, and my face turns bright red. I'm not having this conversation in front of Kirby. The look in Hale's eyes says that he doesn't give a shit what Kirby thinks. But I still do.

Kirby clenches his fists at his sides, fighting to maintain his composure since we're in a professional work setting. "You're a fucking asshole. You can have your pick of women in Chicago, anyone but Brielle. She's like a little sister to me."

Ouch.

Hale's gaze swings over to me. "The truth stings, doesn't it?" he says, his voice soft with a trace of compassion.

Well, fuck him, I don't need his pity. I storm away from the two men, intent on getting the fuck out of here.

On my way toward the exit, Hale's hand closes around mine and he tugs me down a hallway just past the hotel reception.

I yank my hand free from his grasp and spin to face him. "Did you know the entire time?" My heart is pounding and I feel sick and dizzy.

"Yes."

"You live with Kirby. You work with him. And you listened to me whine about him for the past month. Why?"

"That first night I saw you. *Fuck.*" He releases a big exhale and pushes his hands into his hair. "I recognized you right away from a photograph in Kirby's room. I considered walking out right then. I've never worked with a client who I had ties to in my personal life. But I decided to hear you out. You were beautiful. Shy. Nervous. And I wanted to help you."

Hale grasps my arm, but when I look down to glare at his hand, he removes it. "Once we talked, I knew it was never about Kirby. I told you that in the beginning. This was about you. I wanted to help you build your confidence and understand your wants and needs. That was all. Then I was going to walk away. Let him have you, if that's what you really wanted."

His words make no sense.

"Why did you lie about your name?"

"I didn't. It's Cameron Hale. Close friends call me Hale, and when you assumed that was my first name, I didn't correct you."

"And the woman you're buying a house with? Is she your..." The words die in my throat.

"Chrissy's a friend. That's all. We've shared scenes together at the club, but there was never any sexual contact between us."

"Did you do that to her? The bruises?"

"Fucking hell. No!" he roars.

"I don't really know you. How should I know what you're capable of?" Planting my hands on my hips, I meet his dark, stormy eyes.

"The fact that you think I could hurt a woman like that…" His voice breaks, and he doesn't continue.

"How am I supposed to know what to think?"

"You know more than you think you do."

"What does that even mean?" I remember the whispered story I overheard in the ladies' room, and what Kirby told me about Hale's fiancée. Cameron, I remind myself. It's going to be difficult to call him Cameron after thinking of him as Hale for so long. My hunches were right about him from the beginning. He was heartbroken, and that's why he keeps his distance.

"We were done anyway, so what does it matter?" he says, his tone low, defeated.

"You cut our arrangement short. Not me," I challenge.

God, that last night we spent together would forever be burned into my brain. The sweet and tender way we made love, the thoughtfulness behind every gesture he made, the hungry look in his eyes when he studied me in the mirror and lavished me with compliments. In four short weeks, he's come to mean so much to me, and that night we spent together solidified everything.

"You know why I did that," he growls.

"Enlighten me."

"You never once considered calling off this whole game, admitting that Kirby wasn't the man for you." He pauses and I wait for him to continue, but he doesn't. He simply holds me with that icy stare, his look challenging me to disagree.

He's angry—at me—and the injustice of it inflames me. "It doesn't matter now. You lied. You lied about everything. You knew who I was the entire time. How can I trust—" I shake my head. "You're fucking women all over the city of Chicago. None of it matters."

I see that clearly for the first time. Cursing myself, I realize I should have never given him my heart. I feel like a fool for even considering for one second that we could work.

Hale stares at the floor, looking less and less like the domineering man I thought I knew. Still not meeting my eyes, he says, "I haven't taken a client since we began seeing each other."

My heart slams against my ribs as if this moment means everything to me. "You're telling me there was no one else?"

"Just you," he whispers.

Tears spring to my eyes. I have to get out of here. "I can't," I whisper. "I just can't."

Clutching my purse, I let my heels carry me back to the ballroom. I know I owe Kirby an explanation. He was just blindsided, learning that I've been sleeping with his roommate.

I spot him immediately. He's at the same bar where I left him, but it appears he's switched from beer to something stronger. When I get close, I overhear a conversation that wasn't meant for my ears.

"No date tonight?" the man next to Kirby asks.

Kirby shakes his head. "No, my date canceled with the flu, so I invited my friend Brie. She's always free at the last minute."

Anger and disappointment rush through me, and I stop in my tracks as if I've been physically struck. I don't want to be someone's second choice. I've wasted five years of my life, and it's suddenly crystal clear—Kirby is never going to see me as more than a friend. And do I even want him to?

Tears spring to my eyes, and I make my way toward the ladies' room. The last thing I want is for someone to see me cry.

Thankful to find the bathroom empty, I grab a wad of tissue paper just as a sob rips from my throat. I just need to compose myself enough to hail a cab and end this disastrous night. As I sob, I become aware on some level that I'm crying for what will never be with Kirby, and what I can't have with Hale.

The bathroom door opens and when I glance up to the mirror, I see Hale. He locks the bathroom door behind him. My heart pounds out a steady beat as I watch him move confidently toward me.

I dab my cheeks with the tissue and draw in a deep breath, trying to pull it together.

"Come here," he whispers and folds me into his arms.

I don't fight it; I don't even hesitate. I just go to him, molding myself to his firm chest and letting him hold me. His scent washes over me—a mix of crisp cologne and male warmth—and I'm reminded of all the nights I spent in his arms. At his mercy. Obeying his commands.

A desperate sob escapes me, and I push him away. "I can't do this right now."

"Tell me what happened. Why are you in here crying? I figured you'd be in a cab on your way home by now."

That would have been the smart choice. Instead, I went to find Kirby and ease his mind about my involvement with his roommate.

"You were right about Kirby. He's a thoughtless asshole and he doesn't deserve me."

Hale's mouth lifts in a sad smile.

"You knew that all along, didn't you?"

He shrugs. "I had no way of knowing what would happen, but yeah, I had my assumptions."

"Why didn't you tell me?"

"Would you have listened?"

He's right. This was something I had to find out for myself.

He steps closer, tilting my chin up to meet his watchful gaze. "Are you okay?"

I shake my head slowly. "No. But I will be." I'm stronger now than I was before. Even if I don't feel strong in this moment, I know it's true.

"Tell me how to fix this." He brushes his thumb across my cheek, his eyes lingering on mine.

I open my mouth to tell him there's nothing he can do, when he lowers his mouth and kisses me. Softly at first, but when my tongue meets his, his lips crash into mine, his hands landing on my hips, and he grips me tightly to him. He tastes of scotch and Hale, and it's only been a handful of days, but God, how I missed him.

My attraction to this man is off the charts. I'm angry at him for concealing his identity all this time, and I know he doesn't want to pursue anything real, but I can't deny my body's response.

He presses his hips closer, and I feel his huge cock hardening under his tuxedo slacks.

I groan into his mouth and press myself closer, wanting to feel every hard ridge of him.

He pushes me up against the wall and then his hands are under my dress, pulling my panties aside and sweeping his fingers across my wet center.

"Wait..." I say softly.

"What is it?"

"I don't even know what to call you."

"Call me Hale, just like you always have."

His lips crash back into mine, and the intimacy of finally knowing his full name is intoxicating. One finger and then two thrust slowly inside me, and I cry out, weak from both the arousal and the confusion I feel.

"I can't stay away from you, do you understand that?" he murmurs, pressing his hard cock into my belly while his fingers continue sliding in and out.

He knows my body so well that within minutes, I feel myself losing control. His show of dominance is overwhelming. Knowing that he's unable to control the alpha side of him from coming out to play, I'm soaking wet and on the verge of orgasm almost immediately.

"Hale..." I whisper against his mouth.

I'm so close. He bites down on my lower lip and at the same time, presses his thumb to my clit. I come apart, violently, crying out and clutching him for support. He pulls his fingers from me and puts them in his mouth, sucking my juices from them.

"So fucking good," he growls, bringing his mouth to mine again.

He's devouring me, and I'm letting him. I feel his hands working between us, and the clang of his belt buckle as he releases his pants. I want him more than anything, but some part of my brain is screaming at me to stop this.

"It's never been like this before," he whispers.

My legs are shaky, and my brain feels like mud. I'm so confused. My feelings when I'm near him are intense, all consuming, and hot.

Just as I feel the hot flesh of his erection, something snaps into place. It's always been about the sex between us. And look where that's gotten me. My life is spinning out of control. I've been rejected by not one, but two men tonight. Kirby, who I've secretly harbored feelings for for years, and another who's just recently stolen my heart but wants nothing to do with commitment or monogamy.

"S-stop," I stutter, looking up into dark, stormy eyes burning with his arousal.

"We deserve this. This pleasure. This connection," he says, stroking my cheek with his thumb.

There's no way I can give myself to him, not with the million doubts and emotions swirling in my head. I know what I need to do.

Staring into his eyes, I say deliberately, "Peach."

At my firm tone, he pulls back immediately, his jaw tight. "Why?" His expression is broken, confused. I've never used my safe word in all the times we were together.

"You taught me to stand up for myself, to demand more, that sex was an intense experience to be shared between two people. But most of all, you taught me that I'm worth more than this." I gesture to our surroundings—a public bathroom. "I deserve more."

He nods, his face solemn, but his expression unreadable.

Reaching below my dress, I adjust my panties, then grab my purse from the bathroom counter. I leave him with his cock in his hand and look of confusion slashed across his face.

Chapter Twenty-Two

BRIELLE

"Brielle?" The sound of my name in his familiar, low voice immediately sends tingles shooting down my spine. Closing my eyes in shock for just a second, I halt in my tracks on the city sidewalk, trying to suck in a breath but find my chest tight, constricted.

"Hale…" He's all I've thought about this past week since the party. I've seen him in my dreams, heard his voice in my head, and now he's here.

I turn to face him and see he's not alone. An elderly black woman is hanging on to his bicep. She's wearing a floppy purple hat and a bright green scarf. Her lips are painted blood red, and somehow I know this is the sassy woman he's told me about. His nana.

His eyes search out my face, and his mouth lifts in a smile. "You look well...happy."

"I am." For once in my adult life, I really am. I'm carrying a large pizza box—bacon and mushroom, my favorite—and a colorful bouquet of flowers I've bought myself just because.

I wish I could say the same for him. He looks tired, pale, and lifeless. There are dark circles under his eyes and the shadow of a beard dusts his jaw.

"Nana, this is Brielle," he says to the woman at his side.

I glance over at Nana and see an amused expression on her face.

"You're the one who's got him all spun up," she says. It's not a question, and even if it were, I wouldn't know how to answer.

"I'm not spun up," he says.

"He's not himself," she tells me, leaning closer as if we're two old friends swapping recipes.

"It's complicated," I say.

She nods her head, her hat flopping with the movement. "It always is." She reaches out and takes my hand, squeezing it in her own. "He's a difficult man, but he's got a beautiful heart."

I have to practice deep breathing to avoid the tears threatening to spring to my eyes. "Merry Christmas," I murmur.

"It's Christmas Eve, you shouldn't be alone," he says.

Ever since our restroom activities, we've had no connection at all, and I've fought with myself over the need to move on. But now that he's standing in front of me, all masculine and gorgeous, I know I've been fighting a losing battle. My attraction to him, to his heart, hasn't faded at all. His nana is exactly right. He is a difficult man with a beautiful heart. If only he would let me in, things might have been different.

Remembering his question, I shake my head. "I'm not alone. Julie's coming over tonight for dinner." My gaze drops to the pizza box. "Somebody's gotta help me with this. And then in the morning, I'm driving over to my parents' house for

Christmas Day with them and my aunts, uncles, and cousins."

He nods. "We're just heading to church service."

"Nice meeting you, Nana." I nod to her.

"It's good to see you, Brielle," he says.

I swallow the massive lump that's lodged itself in my throat and continue down the sidewalk before I do something completely foolish, like throw myself at him.

• • •

By the time Julie arrives, I've gathered the plates and napkins, poured two glasses of wine, and cued up the Christmas comedy I love.

If only my mood matched the festive atmosphere. I feel like curling up in my bed and crying, but considering that's all I've done for the past week, I know I need to at least try to be social again.

When I let Julie in, she arrives with an armful of gifts.

"You can set them there." I point to my little tabletop tree in the dining room. There are a couple of wrapped gifts for her too. A blue nail polish that she complimented me on, and gift cards to her favorite stores. I've been too distracted to shop much. I hope my family doesn't mind when I show up tomorrow, armed with a Target gift card for everyone.

We sit down with our pizza and wine, and I'm thankful that she's not barraging me with questions about Hale. She knows me well enough by now to understand that I'll talk when I'm ready, but not before.

"Ew. Mushrooms," she says, picking them off of her pizza.

"I forgot you didn't like them. Sorry about that." It just goes to show how distracted I've been.

"Here, you can have extra." She piles the discarded fungi onto my plate. "You and your mushroom fetish."

"I don't have any fetishes." It suddenly strikes me. "Maybe that's the problem."

"Huh?" She takes a slow sip of her wine, waiting for me to continue.

"He was a Dominant, right? I didn't fit into his world. And he probably knew I never would. We never stood a real chance," I say distractedly, talking more to myself than to her at this point.

She scrunches up her brow. "I don't believe that for a second. If things between you two were half as intense as you've said they were, that means something, Brie. Stop discounting yourself. You're not a trained submissive, but you played the role. This is on him. He should have just been honest with you from the beginning."

I take a deep breath. "You're right. I deserve more than a man who can't see my worth. I gave him everything I had in our sessions. I even gave him my heart, though that was never supposed to happen."

She gives me a sympathetic look as she pours more wine into my glass.

I'm starting to see our breakup with more clarity than ever. Besides, if he intended to continue as the

Gentleman Mentor, there isn't a future for us anyway. He said he hadn't taken on any new clients, but that was nowhere near the commitment level I need to fully give myself to him like he requires.

I've learned too much, grown too much in these past several weeks. I just need to keep reminding myself of that and be strong.

Chapter Twenty-Three

BRIELLE

Now that the holiday has passed and things have returned to semi-normal, I know I owe Kirby an explanation. Eager for some closure over this chapter in my life, I ask him to meet me for coffee near my place. I can't risk running into Hale at their apartment.

Once we're seated with steaming drinks in front of us, Kirby looks at me expectantly.

I take a deep breath and blurt it out. "I've loved you for a long time."

His face softens, and he smiles. "I love you too, Brie."

I resist the urge to roll my eyes. Leave it to a man to be totally clueless, with no idea what I'm talking about. "No, Kirby, I hoped for a future with you. I dreamed about more between us."

He clears his throat, his gaze wandering briefly away from mine.

Well, this is awkward.

"I…I don't know what to say," he finally says. "I've never seen you that way." His voice is soft, as if he's trying to break the news to me gently.

"I know that. And I'm happy to say that I finally figured that out and moved on. I wanted to tell you about Cameron. I didn't want you to hear it from anyone else."

He nods, his jaw tight. It's clear he's angry at us both for hiding this from him.

"We met at an online dating site. I've been sleeping with him for the past month, but I had no idea he was your roommate."

"Wow. I guess I'm a little stunned. Are you guys dating?"

I shake my head. "No. We had a physical relationship, and I hoped it would grow into something more. But that was foolish thinking, I guess."

He nods as if something has just clicked into place. "He's been miserable ever since that night of the law firm holiday party. Did you guys break things off?"

I nod. "Yes. I haven't seen him since then."

Well, aside from that one brief run-in on the sidewalk where I thought my heart was going to implode. Watching him cradle his nana's frail hand in the crook of his arm as he led her down the street, bending low so he could hear what the small woman said—it was all heart-melting. I always figured *nana* was just a term of endearment for a biological grandmother. Knowing he laid claim to her as his own was even more touching.

"No wonder he's been a dick," Kirby says, shaking his head as if this explains everything.

I want to ask more, to question him and find out what's been going on with Hale, but whatever he tells me will only make this harder. I need to move on.

"Are you okay with everything?" I ask. "I just want to make sure we're good."

"Of course we are, ladybug." He takes my hand and squeezes.

The role Kirby has filled in my life is coming to a close. We'll always be friends, but I don't *need* him; I no longer yearn for his love and approval like I once did.

I experienced the real thing with Hale. And I want to figure out what is next for me.

• • •

Late one afternoon a few days later, my intercom buzzes, and since I'm not expecting company, I'm curious about who it could be.

When I open my front door, there's no one there, but my gaze is drawn downward. A ripe, plump peach sits atop a manila file folder. Glancing down the hall, I see there's no one there, but I know it has to be Hale.

I pick up the fruit and bring it to my nose, then inhale. The scent is fragrant and wonderful. After picking the folder, I shuffle inside my apartment, shutting the door behind me. I set the peach down on the table and remove the stack of documents from the folder, spreading them out before me as my mind works to make sense of what I'm seeing.

There's a handwritten note on top of the first page.

This is me.

Cameron Alexander Hale had concealed his name and identity from me, and it appears he's now an open book. His résumé lists the name of the law firm he works at, along with where he interned and his alma mater. Next are bank statements showing a modest checking account and a sizeable savings account. His immunization records, showing that he's up-to-date on all vaccines and gets his flu shot every year. Performance reviews from his last three years of work.

In awe, I continue leafing through the pages, wondering how much time and effort it took him to pull this all together. I stop when my fingers touch a glossy photograph of a woman. His ex-fiancée, Tara, the note says. I look down into her dark brown eyes, hating that she was the one responsible for damaging this man, making him feel the need to guard himself so completely.

Taking a deep breath, I set the photograph aside. This isn't about her. This is about Hale wanting to share a piece of himself with me, however scary that might be for him.

There's a tattered paperback copy of *A New Earth* by Eckhart Tolle, which I'm guessing from the well-worn spine is one of his favorite books. I flip it open and see a few passages have been highlighted with blue marker.

"The past has no power over the present moment."

"Only the truth of who you are, if realized, will set you free."

Overwhelmed, I sink into the chair as the words on all the pages before me start to blur together. There's an obituary from his hometown newspaper that speaks of his parents in the past tense. I imagine this was one of the more painful pieces of his story to include. It took courage and trust for him to leave this packet for me, just as it took courage and trust for me to submit to him.

There are pages and pages to sift through, and at the bottom, an envelope filled with cash. A note tucked inside says he's returning the money I paid him for his services.

Unsure what to do with all of this information, I recall a whispered conversation between him and Chrissy, the woman I sold that house to.

"Is she someone you know from Crave?" Chrissy asked him.

"No, nothing like that." He scoffed at the idea.

At the time, I was so overcome with confusion and heartache that I dismissed it. But now I'm curious what Crave is, and soon I'm Googling "Chicago + Crave" and scrolling through the search results.

I know the moment I've stumbled across it. Crave is an exclusive BDSM club in the heart of Chicago. I click to visit their website and find I can't look away from my screen.

Chapter Twenty-Four

BRIELLE

Gone is the unsure, timid girl who first met Hale in the jazz club that night. It's not lost on me that the first time we met, he brought me so close to his club, yet kept me so far away from his life all that time.

Radiating confidence all the way from my stiletto heels to the cups of my lacy bra, I take a deep breath and straighten my shoulders. I've chosen a black leather miniskirt and a silky blouse in the most beautiful color of soft peach. I feel pretty and calm.

"You look really nice tonight," Kirby says, admiring me fondly.

"Thank you."

"Are you sure you're ready for this?"

"Absolutely."

Hale has no idea I'm coming tonight. I can't even begin to imagine what his reaction will be when he sees me. When I researched Crave online, I saw that tonight they are having a New Year's Eve party. The club is rarely open to guests, so it seemed like a sign that I was meant to come here.

After the doorman checks our IDs and we pay a steep entry fee, Kirby and I enter a large room with chairs and sofas scattered around a fireplace, and a bar area for mingling. I'm not sure why, but I was expecting something more sinister. It's more like a lounge with darkly sensual music, and lighting designed to make you feel hidden in shadows. There are two women playing out a scene in the wide-open play space at the room's center.

For every exhibitionist, there's a voyeur, I suppose. Something tells me that's just the tip of the iceberg of what I might see tonight. Transfixed, I watch as the woman holding a burning red candle tilts it and lets a trail of wax drip onto her partner's cleavage. I'm reminded of the scented candle and the beautiful fragrance that floated around Hale and me as he pushed me to my limits time and time again.

"Brie?" Kirby asks, drawing me back to the moment. "Everything okay?"

"Of course. It's just a little overwhelming."

He nods, his eyes widening as a stunning blond woman wearing only a blue G-string and knee-high boots struts past, her perky breasts bouncing as she passes us. She's gorgeous and seems to know exactly where she's headed, moving with purpose toward an unknown destination.

My stomach sinks as I realize for the first time that Hale may not be here alone. It's a feeling that haunts me as Kirby takes my hand and leads me toward the bar.

Before we can place our order, I spot Chrissy, my client and Hale's friend. She's headed straight toward us.

"I never expected to see you here," she says, greeting me warmly with a hug.

"We were up for an adventure tonight. This is my friend Kirby."

As they shake hands, I hide my smile as Kirby struggles to keep his eyes from wandering south. Chrissy is dressed in gorgeous vintage lingerie—a black lace teddy, stockings, garters, and black satin gloves.

"How are you enjoying your new home?" I ask.

"I love it. I made my first Christmas dinner there and had half of the club over."

I wonder if Hale spent Christmas there, and if he did, would that make me jealous. I decide it doesn't matter. Besides, somehow I picture him spending the holiday with his nana. Probably unwrapping boxes of scarves and sweaters knit just for him.

"What do you think of the club?" she asks.

"It's...good. So far, I mean, we haven't seen much yet."

My gaze wanders back over to the public display of feminine dominance and submission, which has advanced to the Domme applying a nipple clamp to one breast while she licks at the other with her tongue. My heart quickens as I watch.

I turn back toward Chrissy, eager to find out if he's here or not. I don't want this bold experiment to be all for nothing. "Is Hale here?"

She nods, but her expression gives nothing away. "He's with Reece. In the lounge." She points toward an arched doorway that leads into another dimly lit room.

I don't care what the lounge is; I only want to know who the hell Reece is and what the fuck she's doing with my man. I pull in a deep lungful of air and straighten my shoulders.

"Kirby, would you like a personalized tour?" Chrissy asks.

He turns to me. "Will you be okay, ladybug?"

I nod. "Yes, go. Have fun."

They stride off toward the other end of the room, and all my thoughts of ordering a drink are gone. Now the only thing that matters is getting into the lounge to see with my own eyes what he's up to.

The stilettos on my feet carry me closer and closer, the clicking sound they make matching the hard and fast pounding of my heart. I stop in the entryway, my eyes fighting to adjust. The room is even dimmer than the main area I've come from. The low, sensual music thumps softly in the background. There are a few couples and small groups sitting together, quietly talking and sipping drinks, but Hale's not one of them.

Then I notice two men seated in the far corner of the room, their heads tipped down as if they're discussing something serious. Instinctively, even though I can't make out either of their features, I know the man on the left is Hale. My sweet, lost man. Only when I'm standing directly before them do I realize that it's rude of me to interrupt them like this.

"Brielle…" Hale stands suddenly, his eyes flashing with confusion. "What are you doing here?"

I knew seeing me at his BDSM club would come as a shock. I only hope it's a pleasant surprise and not an unwelcome one.

"Kirby brought me."

His expression sours. "I see." I open my mouth to explain that it's not at all like that when Hale gestures to the man beside him. "This is Reece. He owns the club."

Reece rises to his feet, and dear God, this man is huge. At least six and a half feet tall with shoulders so broad he could easily pass for an NFL player. As he towers over me, his dark, imposing good looks render me momentarily speechless. "You're stunning, angel. Are you here to play?"

"Back the fuck off, Reece," Hale growls.

I can't help the rush of pink staining my cheeks. Even if I'm not interested in Reece, his attention is flattering.

"Welcome to Crave," Reece says, lifting my hand to his mouth and placing a kiss in the center. "I hope you find what you're looking for."

"I do too." My eyes wander over to Hale's, and a rush of heat tingles low in my belly.

"Fuck." Reece presses his earpiece to his ear, obviously listening to bad news. "There's a woman at the front door saying she knows me."

Hale shrugs. "What's the problem? A lot of women in this city know you."

"Yeah, but she says we grew up together, and I have a bad feeling about who it might be."

"Let's roll, brother. Do you need me?" Hale asks him.

I get the unmistakable feeling that he wants as far away from me as possible. And who could blame him? I just told him that I'm here with another man. But all I need is a few seconds to explain…

"No," Reece says, his eyes wandering to mine and his expression softening. "You stay here and entertain your *friend*." Reece stalks off, but I hear him call *dibs*, to which Hale mutters a low curse under his breath. It's so interesting seeing this side of him—in his club, with his male friend.

I merely stand here, taking it all in and trying to piece everything together.

Hale finally turns to face me again. "I don't know what to say, Brielle. I don't understand why you're here."

"I got the file you left for me."

"And what...you just show up here? No phone call, no text, nothing for days."

"I wanted to show you that I'm here. You, this lifestyle, it doesn't scare me."

He nods once, his expression stern. "And Kirby?"

"I told him everything. About me and you. About the feelings I had for him."

He picks up a glass of whiskey from the table and downs the remainder of his drink.

"I told him I once wished for a future with him, but not anymore. I've grown. I've changed, and I want different things now."

"What kind of things?"

I shrug, playing innocent. "Things that a Dom demands of his sub."

"I've been drinking, Brielle," he warns, his tone low.

"I don't care." I gesture to the chairs that he and Reece vacated. "Can we sit down for a minute and talk?"

He takes my hand and guides me to the plush leather armchair, sitting down across from me.

"Why did you show me all of that?" I ask.

"Because that's me. That was everything. My past, the losses and pain I've experienced, it's made me the man that I am, and I don't share that with people, but I was worried that you'd fallen for the Gentleman Mentor. It's happened before," he adds with a faraway look in his eyes, and I know there's a story there I'll be digging into later.

"I needed you to see the real me," he says, "warts and all, and decide if I was what you wanted. I want to keep you for myself, leave all that shit, the mentoring behind. I want you. But I wasn't sure you even knew what you wanted. You'd held on to that fantasy of you and Kirby for so long that—" He shakes his head, looking down into his empty glass.

I place my hand on his knee. I've never seen Hale like this. He's vulnerable and exposed in a way he's never been before, and it scares me, but I like it.

"I didn't fall for the Gentleman Mentor. I fell for *you*. I fell for the careful way you lifted my hair from my neck to kiss that sensitive spot below my ear. The feeling of your lips at my temple, the sweet and wicked things you whispered to give me the confidence I needed to soar. I fell for the sexy, disciplined control you maintain, the sweet way you are with your nana, all the real stuff that makes you *you*."

His gaze softens and latches onto mine. "I wasn't as good as I thought at hiding myself from you."

I shrug. "Not even a little bit." We're silent for a few minutes, each happy to drink in the other's presence. "You didn't have to return the money," I finally add.

"I didn't feel right keeping it." He leans closer. "Would you like a tour of the club?"

Eagerly, I nod. "Unless we're going to run into any of your old girlfriends."

"I haven't dated in years, Brielle. I thought you knew that."

"I guess there's still a lot I'm fuzzy on."

"Let me clear a few things up for you. Come with me." He rises to his feet and offers me his hand.

As we exit the lounge via a back hallway, I snag a glass of champagne from a passing waiter, knowing I very well might need a dose of liquid courage.

Chapter Twenty-Five

HALE

Having Brielle inside Crave makes me feel possessive and territorial in a way I've never experienced before. As we climb the stairs to the second level, Doms openly admire her. Even a few submissives lift their eyes to inspect her, silently wishing they look half as poised and beautiful as she does tonight. It makes me proud to have her on my arm, yet part of me wants to lock her away in a private room, away from the lecherous eyes that follow us.

I skipped the tour of the first floor, because it's mostly just a lounge and bar meant for mingling, along with a public play area, which I'm sure she saw when she came in. The second floor is where the real action takes place.

"Where did you leave Kirby?" I ask, suddenly remembering she said she came with him.

"With Chrissy."

I nod. "He'll be fine then." Chrissy only plays with real Doms, and since Kirby doesn't even come close to fitting that bill, they're probably just having a drink. "Come here, I want to show you something."

We reach the first room, and I stop in the hall to face her. "If anything you see bothers you, just squeeze my hand, okay?"

She nods, and I push open the heavy steel door to the dungeon-inspired playroom. Hooks stud the floors, walls, and ceiling. A padded bench and an iron cross with restraints provide play areas, and they're both currently occupied.

Given that New Year's Eve is one of the biggest party nights, the club is packed with many people dressed in fetish gear. Brielle's eyes are wide as she takes in everything. She's quiet and almost contemplative about what she's seeing, but she never once squeezes my hand as I guide her from room to room.

We only briefly tour the sterile hospital-themed room where a man is using a violet wand on his patient. Brielle flinches when the spark of electricity leaps from the end of the wand and onto the woman's bare pussy.

"What is that?"

"The wand produces erotic electric stimulation. It provides a warm tingling sensation, but used on a low setting, doesn't have the power to produce real pain."

Brielle sags in relief beside me, but I can tell this is outside her comfort zone. Mine too, if I'm honest. It takes a lot of skill and restraint for a Dom to learn how to use the tool properly.

Once we're back in the hallway, I lean down to whisper near her ear. "How are you doing?"

She gives me a tight nod. "It's all very...enlightening."

I nod in agreement. "Have you seen enough?" This scene was a little overwhelming, even for an experienced Dom like me. I tend to opt for privacy and sensuous scenes, not the public, extreme play that is going on inside these rooms tonight.

"Which room is your favorite?"

The idea of getting her alone and out of that miniskirt has my cock hardening already. "This way."

We turn the corner to a less busy area of the club. The ultra-private Pandora rooms can be used for private scenes.

I find a door with a green light, meaning that it's available for use, and turn to face Brielle. "Are you sure you're game for all this?"

"There's only one thing I want."

"What's that?"

"The other times we were together were about me. You taught me to be confident and made me feel desirable, but tonight I want to see what *you* like."

"I like anything that involves you naked, sweetheart."

She shakes her head, frowning at me. "I'm serious. No more going easy on me. I mean it."

"And you're sure that's what I've been doing?" Something about seeing her in this environment amuses me. I'm practically fucking giddy, and I can't help but tease her a little.

"Yes. I...I think so," she says. "I want to learn your preferences. Please."

I take a deep breath, my cock once again flexing against my zipper. "Are you sure that's what you want?"

"Absolutely."

"Very well." It's like she's flipped a switch inside me. "I need you to be sure."

"I am." She straightens her shoulders, refusing to back down.

"And you remember your safe word?"

"Peach."

"Good girl." I point to the door we're standing in front of. "This is a private room with a locking door."

"So it'll be just us?"

"If that's what you want."

She swallows, her throat working with the effort. "I trust you."

"Do you know what it means if I ask you to present yourself?"

Her answering gaze is inquisitive. "No, sir," she admits after a beat.

I nod toward the door. "You are to go inside and undress completely. Then I want you to kneel with your forehead on the floor, so that your ass and pussy are displayed for me. Is that understood?"

"Yes, sir."

"We never fully outlined your limits."

"I trust you."

I can see her pulse strumming almost violently in her neck. As much as it pains me, in order to really push Brielle tonight, I need to call in some backup. I saw her reaction to Reece earlier, and I'm going to use it to my full advantage.

She wants to know what I like, and what I really enjoy is taking a sub so far outside herself that she's fully reliant on me. I want to push her so she's just beyond the edge of her comfort zone. It's only then that she has fully given herself to me. And I need to feel that from her tonight. I need to know she's really mine; it's the only way to completely let her in.

I open the door, turning the light to red as Brielle goes inside. The private rooms are all nice, but this is one of my favorites. It's a large room with a four-poster bed covered by a single white sheet. The only light in the room comes from a half dozen candles that burn in sparkling crystal dishes across the room. It's a beautiful environment, made even more stunning by the beautiful woman who's stepped into the room.

I close the door softly behind her, giving us both a moment to prepare for what is sure to be the most intense scene we've ever shared.

After several minutes, I'm ready, and I can practically feel the anticipation and nervous energy flowing off of Brielle, even through the closed door.

I open the door and find her exactly as I've instructed. She's kneeling on the soft wool rug in the center of the room. Her forehead is resting on the carpet, her ass is upturned toward me so that my view is of her perfect pussy and little pink asshole. My cock jumps to attention as all the blood in my body pumps south, hard and fast.

"You've presented yourself beautifully," I say, so she knows it's me who's just entered the room.

"Thank you, sir," she murmurs.

"I've brought you a surprise. Are you ready for him?"

"Him?" she squeaks, all the muscles in her body tightening.

I've called Reece for help with this scene. "Is that okay?" I ask.

After several moments, I hear her small voice again. "I trust you, sir."

"That's a good girl."

I open the door and watch as her breathing grows shallow at the sound of distinctly male footsteps across the floor. I can't even begin to imagine Brielle's mind space right now, but I've pushed her further than ever before, and so far she's accepting of it.

I won't let Reece lay a hand on her, and he knows that, but something about her reaction earlier, both to him and to the couples putting on a public show, tells me this is just the kind of thing to push her to the next level.

"Would you look at how pretty that is, Reece?"

It's the first time I've spoken his name, and my use of it is deliberate. I want her to picture two tall, powerful Doms standing over her nude body, both of us rock hard. She holds all the power, and the way she relaxes and pushes her ass out just a fraction more tells me she knows this.

"She's fucking gorgeous." Reece's voice is rough and low. He might be an experienced Dom, but even he can see how beautiful, and unique this woman is in all her naked glory.

"And she's learning to be a good little submissive. Presenting her tight little asshole and pussy to us like that." I have to fight to maintain the composure in my voice, that's how much this scene is affecting me. Blood hums through my veins, and I'm intoxicated by her.

"She looks good enough to eat," he comments.

I glance over at him, and when I see a dark, hungry look in his eyes, I shoot him an evil glare. *Dream on, fucker.*

I walk closer to Brielle, leaning down beside her to stroke my fingertips lightly over her spine. "You're doing beautifully," I whisper.

Normally I wouldn't dole out compliments just yet, but this isn't her world. This is totally new for her, and she could easily pass for a pro with how well she's handling this.

"Tell me how you feel."

"Nervous," she admits and then she adds softly, "Alive."

"That's perfect." My fingertips follow the graceful curve of her spine, down to her ass. "Open for me just a little more. Ease your knees apart."

She does, and when I lower my fingers to her sex, I find her soaking wet. I push one finger inside, loving the feel of her tight walls clinging to me.

"Damn, baby. This little pussy is drenched to perfection. You like having two Doms hard and aching at just the sight of you?"

She makes a small noise of pleasure and pushes her ass back to take my finger deeper.

"Greedy thing." I remove my hand and spank her ass, giving her a sharp swat.

Brielle moans at the contact, but doesn't even flinch.

She took her spanking so well, that I reward her with two fingers deep inside her.

I look at Reece, who looks beyond impressed at how well she's doing. I told him training them was the fun part. Something tells me maybe now, he'll believe me.

"Fucking hell, she looks tight," he growls.

Pride blooms within me. "She is. Tightest pussy I've ever felt." She fits around me perfectly as I pump in and out, and her hot cunt sucks at my fingers.

Little whimpering mewls escape her as if she's trying to stay quiet but can't hold back.

"Hmm. Should I let him have a taste?"

Brielle squeaks in surprise, her body flinching.

"Do you need to use your safe word, Brielle?"

"I..." She hesitates, breathing heavily. "Just you. Please."

Of course I'll be the only one tasting her. If another man licking her pussy while I watched was what she really wanted, I don't know if I could deny her, but it pleases me immensely to hear her say we're on the exact same page. It'll be just us tonight. Which is exactly as it should be.

I continue my movements inside her, and I can feel her getting close. Knowing her body as well as I do, I can read all of her signs. "When you come, it'll be for my eyes only," I tell her.

"Yes, sir," she says, grinding her ass back against me again.

Naughty thing. She's trying to taunt me in front of Reece, topping from the bottom. And damn if she doesn't have me wrapped around her little finger. I want nothing more than to let her explode all over my hand, but I force myself to stop and stand.

"I think it's time to get down to business. On your feet, peach."

Brielle rises to her knees first and gazes up at me. We've barely begun our scene, and already her eyes have that glassy, faraway look in them. She gets to her feet and stands before us, completely bare and unashamed. There's no tremor in her stance, and her chin is lifted high. Knowing that she holds all the power in this exchange, she's confident and calm. God, she's grown so much since we began. It's incredible.

Her gaze drops to the front of my pants and then swings over to Reece's next.

Yes, you've brought two big men to their breaking point. Happy, sweetheart?

"Time to go, Reece," I tell him. I needed to push Brielle completely out of her comfort zone tonight, and after I saw the way she reacted to the others at the club, I knew she was intrigued with the idea of being watched. But I never intended for him to actually participate. Her perfection is reserved for me alone.

Reece gives a tight nod, his eyes on Brielle. "You're fucking gorgeous, angel. Enjoy the rest of your night at the club. If I can ever be of service, please let me know."

Reece leaves, and then it's just the two of us.

"Was that okay, peach?" It was a bold move on my part, calling for a mid-scene check-in. I need to know that she's okay before we continue.

"I never expected it. It was…different."

"And you're ready to continue?"

"Yes." There's no hesitation, no question.

"Good. Come here and take out my cock."

Brielle walks closer, her breasts jiggling as she moves. I can feel pre-come leaking from the end of my cock. If I don't get her mouth on me soon, I'm going to explode.

She releases my button and tugs down the zipper, and then her hands are inside my boxers, her delicate fingers curling around my shaft. I groan and stifle a curse.

"How's this, sir?" she asks, her eyes full of fire.

"Down on your knees, pet. I want to be in your mouth."

She sinks to her knees and frees me the rest of the way from my pants, letting them fall to my ankles. Then she plants her hand at the base and brings her lips to my tip, licking the head lightly. Zings of pleasure shoot down into my balls.

"Deeper," I growl.

She opens and takes me into the warmth of her mouth, sucking noises punctuating the silence around us. Her hand strokes up and down, following the path of her tongue.

She's swallowing me down her throat, and I'm seconds away from coming when I pull myself free.

"Fuck." I stroke her hair, tucking it back behind her ears. My cock is so hard and primed, it aches, but I want to be inside her when I come.

She smiles up at me, her lips swollen and damp.

"Come here, beautiful." I lift her in my arms and walk us over to the dresser. When I sit her on the top, it's the perfect height for bringing us together. "I can't wait any longer."

I push her knees apart and step between them, kissing her deeply while my thumb strokes her clit. She moans into my mouth, her tongue tangling with mine. Right when she's on the brink of orgasm, I push inside in one swift thrust.

Brielle comes apart, clawing at my shoulders and crying out loudly.

My thumb doesn't stop stroking her swollen clit as her walls slam down around me. "That's it, peach. Come all over me. Just let go."

I continue rocking in and out of her, and when I look down between us, I see my cock coated in her slick heat.

Her breathing is coming hard and fast, and her eyes are glazed over with lust. I pull myself free and carry her over to the bed, laying her down gently.

I'm worried I've pushed her too far tonight. That being here, inside this club, inviting another man into the room, might have been all too much. She's trembling all over, and I grab a throw blanket from the cabinet, covering her up and cuddling her to my chest. Once she catches her breath, she blinks up at me.

"Why didn't you finish?" She looks down at my still semi-hard erection.

"Your well-being comes first. You were shaking like a leaf."

She gives me a coy look. "I'd just come harder than I have in my entire life. That didn't mean I needed to stop."

She reaches for me and strokes me lightly. I'm fully hard again in an instant.

"Are you sure you don't need a minute?" I grunt.

"Positive."

I kiss her deeply as the unmistakable feeling that this woman was made for me crashes through me.

"Besides, you're supposed to be showing me what *you* like, remember?"

"Are you sure about that?" I know exactly what I want.

She nods.

"Then turn over."

With a quizzical look on her delicate features, she rolls onto her stomach.

I grab a pillow and lift her, placing it under her hips, then grab my toy bag from beside the door. I don't have our candle because I didn't expect to see her tonight, but a Dom never leaves home without his bag. I'm like a Boy Scout that way. You never know when you might need to instruct a fellow Dom on the proper use of a double-short-tail flogger.

When I return to the bed, Brielle is resting with her cheek on the mattress, watching me closely. "Wh-what are you going to do?"

"Just try and relax for me, okay?" I consider blindfolding her, but then decide I'm introducing her to enough new sensations tonight; no need to throw that into the mix too. Besides, I want to see her eyes and her expression when I take her.

I grab some lubricant from my bag and set it on the bed beside me.

"Remember this?" It's the vibrator I used on her in the condo she was showing clients.

"Fondly," she says.

I tuck it back inside its case and put it in the bag. "Too bad we won't be using it then." I smirk. "Let's try this one." It's a Jimmy Jane Form Two. A double-pronged love device, one of my favorites because it produces an almost immediate orgasm. It will be perfect to tease her with and to test her control.

"Is that a plug?" she asks, noting the little toy in my hand with its smooth end and flared base.

I don't need to spell it out for her. My cock is big; her ass is tight. It's simple mechanics. "It'll help make sure you're ready for me."

She watches me curiously, but doesn't say anything.

"Up on your knees a little bit for me, sweetheart."

She grants me the access I desire, her butt lifting just slightly off the bed.

I place the vibrator under her pelvis and turn it on. Her entire body jolts in surprise.

"Holy shit!"

Raising an eyebrow at her. "Everything okay down there?"

"What is this thing?" she gasps, her hands already clawing at the sheets.

"Just a little toy to make sure you're ready for me."

Standing at the edge of the bed, I take my time to undress completely while Brielle watches me, her eyes fluttering with the pleasurable buzz against her clit.

She moans low in her throat, and her body trembles. Her pussy is glistening, and it takes everything I have to restrain myself.

"Don't come without me, sweetheart," I warn.

"Hale..." she pants, nearing the edge of orgasm already.

"Maybe I overestimated your self-control."

Once I'm fully undressed, I take my cock in my hand and begin stroking myself slowly from base to tip. Brielle's eyes cloud over with lust as her gaze zeros in on my movements, and her entire body shudders.

"I'm going to come..." she moans.

"Don't you dare."

"Hale!" she shouts, her thighs trembling with the effort of holding back.

I pull the vibrator from beneath her and change it to a lower setting while Brielle fights to catch her breath.

"Naughty girl. I should spank you, but instead I'm going to fuck your ass, because I can't wait any longer."

Picking up the plug, I warm it in my hands and add some lubricant before placing it flush against her back opening.

"What's your safe word, Brielle?" I ask softly, leaning over her to kiss her earlobe.

"Peach."

"And when should you use it?"

"If I want all play to stop," she answers, still breathless.

"Good girl."

I place the vibrator back in its magic spot, the low hum barely audible.

"Is that more manageable?" I ask.

"Yes," she moans.

"Good. Now just breathe and relax for me."

I push the plug inside her, feeling her sharp inhale at the foreign contact. But Brielle doesn't fight it, doesn't flinch away. She looks gorgeous with my plug in her ass, and I admire her bravery. After I've given her the chance to get used to it stretching her, I remove it, then coat myself with more lubricant, wanting this to be as comfortable as possible for her.

Soon, I'm gripping both of her ass cheeks and slowly, ever so slowly, sinking inside her inch by delicious inch. She's so warm and fits so snugly around my dick that I immediately want to explode.

"Fuck."

I know I have to go easy with her, but sweat breaks out across my back and neck with the effort of holding myself still while she adjusts.

"You good, sweetheart?" I ask, needing to hear her words.

"Yes, it's...different, and I feel full, but I like it."

Brielle lies still, breathing deep breaths in and out, just like I told her. Her submission is so beautiful, it warms me.

"That's it, you're doing great." I place my hand on her lower back and set an easy rhythm. We're so physically connected, I can feel the little vibrations humming through her.

"Hale..." she moans.

I think she's going to tell me that she's going to come again, but what comes out of her mouth next totally shocks me.

"Yes?"

"I want…I want to take charge, like you showed me."

Fucking hell. "Go for it, baby." I still my movements, letting her take the floor.

And soon, she's the one fucking me, impaling herself on my cock over and over as her round ass wiggles against me.

I reach down and squeeze the base of my dick, trying not to come yet, but I can't last. Her pussy is soaking wet, and I can feel her slick heat on my balls.

"Are you close, peach?"

"Yeah…I'm there," she moans, her movements becoming erratic.

Thank fuck. I let myself go, hot streams of semen jetting out of me just as she gives a tight cry and collapses on the bed, utterly spent.

Chapter Twenty-Six

BRIELLE

After we made love, Hale made sure I was okay, giving me small sips from a bottle of water and covering me up with blankets. But now, as I'm resting on the bed, feeling sated and happy, his features are twisted with confusion.

"If tonight was too much, if I'm too much...fuck," he curses.

I place my hand over his heart. I can read it all over him. He's questioning if he pushed me too far, if his dominant nature is too much for me to handle.

"You don't have to change for me." *You don't have to make me love you, because I already do.* I hope my gaze on his communicates everything I need it to, because my words are failing me.

"You're amazing," he says, gazing at me thoughtfully. "I never thought I'd want this again. And I do. I want you. Forever."

I know this is absolutely huge for him. After his fiancée obliterated his trust, for him to open his heart up to a future with me is…indescribable. There are a million things I want to tell him, but he's not through.

"You're everything to me; you got under my skin right from our first lesson and you never let go. And then seeing how perfectly you responded tonight…" He makes a low sound of appreciation under his breath. "You're everything I've ever wanted and more, sweetheart."

"Hale, I…" I'm trying to form into words everything he means to me as tears spring to my eyes.

"Shh. Let me finish. You asked what I wanted tonight. And now there's just one thing left that I want."

He places his hand on my cheek, and his thumb strokes my skin. This man's sexual appetite is insatiable, and I'm beginning to question how I'm going to keep up, when he leans in close and presses his lips to mine.

"I want your heart," he whispers.

I kiss his full, soft lips, my heart soaring with happiness. "You already have it," I whisper back.

"Forever," he says.

"Do you promise?" I don't think he's toying with me, but I can't stomach the thought of losing him again.

"You belong with me. We both felt it from day one, and we both fought it, each of us for different reasons. But that's done now. No more fighting. I just want to love you."

A single tear slips from my eye, and his thumb catches it on my cheek. "I want that too." It may not be the path I thought I wanted, but being with Hale, submitting to him, letting go of everything, it's a deeper love than I ever imagined. It takes more trust and courage than I ever knew I had. I am blessed beyond measure, and I don't even want to think about what my life would be like today if I hadn't taken that first crazy step and e-mailed him.

"Now let's go home," he says. "I want to hold you all night and wake up with you in the morning."

That sounds perfect to me. It was something denied me during our lessons.

We dress quickly and hurry from the club, stopping for a brief, but passionate kiss when the clock strikes midnight and confetti rains down on us.

I'm so overcome with emotion at the promise of this new year and new beginning, that Hale has to help me outside and into his car.

Epilogue

TO: *Brielle @bookworm92*

FROM: *Cameron Hale @thedominantgentleman*

SUBJECT: *Peach*

Male. Late 20s. Dominant. Stubborn, but loving.
Well hung.
Fucks like a goddamn porn star.
Looking for a wife.
What do you say, peach? Be mine forever?
xx,
Hale

TO: *Cameron Hale @thedominantgentleman*

FROM: *Brielle @bookworm92*

SUBJECT: RE: *Peach*

Yes!!!!!! Of course I will you big, silly man. I'm keeping you forever.

Want More Hale?

Visit www.kendallryanbooks.com to purchase
your own luxury soy candle that's custom-scented to
match Hale's. You will love it!

Sinfully Mine

LESSONS WITH THE DOM BOOK TWO

A stand-alone romance about BDSM club owner,
Reece

I have one rule for myself. Don't fuck the patrons. But as the owner of a BDSM club, that rule is harder to abide by than you might realize. It becomes even more difficult when my best friend's little sister arrives at my club, lonely and confused, seeking refuge from her ex. I know I could help her, teach her, and build that quiet confidence she's lost, if only she doesn't break me first.

Read on for a sneak preview of *Sinfully Mine*.

Sneak Preview of Sinfully Mine

CHAPTER ONE

REECE

She's standing here as if she didn't shatter my entire world six years ago.

Blinking my eyes against what I'm sure is a mirage, or maybe too much scotch, I address the gorgeous woman standing demurely before me. "Macey?"

I'd recognize her anywhere, but this isn't the girl I remember. I haven't seen her in years, and she's grown up. A lot. Her features are sharper, and she's lost the childlike roundness to her face. But mostly it's the look in her eyes that's different—as if she's seen too much of the world, and had to cut her own path through it. She's harder, edgier, wiser...but she's still Macey. And my heart is beating like a fucking drum at the sight of her.

"Hi, Reece." Her tone is guarded, as are her eyes.

I fell in love with her when I was nineteen and she was just sixteen. I knew it was wrong; she was my best friend's little sister. But when she lost her parents in a plane crash that year, I was the one she turned to for comfort, and our friendship evolved into a relationship.

Of course, my best friend, Hale, doesn't know any of this because it ended when she went away to college. It had to. Macey was always destined for more, and leaving was exactly what she needed, even if she took a part of me with her.

Despite the fact that we're standing in the busy lounge of my BDSM club, Crave, I'm immediately transported back to her quiet, dim bedroom six years ago. I was twenty, with all the wants and needs of a man, and she was just an inexperienced girl of eighteen...

• • •

Macey's panties were wet, and her chest heaved up and down with her quick, shallow breaths. "Are you sure about this?" I asked her.

"I'm sure," she said, her voice small, but steady.

Her white cotton underwear left little to the imagination, since the now-damp fabric clung to the inviting pink skin underneath. I'd been rubbing her clit through her panties, unwilling to undress her completely because I knew what would happen once I did. Her knees were spread apart, her thin tank top unable to conceal the firm peaks of her nipples. She was beautiful—a lesson in contradictions. Shy, but uninhibited. Inexperienced, yet eager.

She was close, whimpering softly as my fingers worked on her. My cock was so hard it ached, and all the blood pumping south was clouding my judgment. Continuing to caress her, I used my free hand to release my belt and open my pants. Taking myself in my hand, I pumped my cock up and down, needing a release so fucking badly it hurt.

Macey and I both released a shuddering breath at the same moment. Her gaze was glued to my jerky movements, and I could feel all of her muscles trembling.

"Do you have a condom?" she asked, a slight tremor to her words.

I had two condoms in my wallet, and as much as I wanted her, I was also scared out of my mind. I'd never slept with a woman I loved. Up until this moment, sex been a meaningless physical act meant to quiet the need raging inside me, nothing more than joyless weekend hookups with girls whose names I wouldn't recall in the morning.

But Macey wasn't just the girl I'd grown to love, she was also my best friend's little sister and a virgin—a combination that was completely off-limits. So why was I in her bed with my cock in my hand?

I didn't answer her about the condom—not because I couldn't—but because in that moment, the only thing I wanted was to watch her come again. As I leaned down to take her mouth, her greedy tongue met mine, sucking hard as she lifted her hips slightly off the bed, pressing herself into my touch. My hand slid up and down my shaft, and I knew I was going to come soon. I kissed a path down her neck to her collarbone, making my way down her body past the dip in her belly until I settled between her thighs.

Lifting the fabric of her panties to the side, I exposed her delicate pink flesh. She was beautiful. I'd always insisted that her panties stay on while we fooled around. It was my one nonnegotiable rule, a small thing to ease my guilt. Macey opened her mouth to protest until she felt my tongue lap at her clit, and then she gave a short whimper and buried her hands in my hair, tugging me closer as her head dropped back on the pillow.

I chuckled against her skin, loving the taste of her. She tasted even better than I could have imagined. And her cunt smelled so fucking good, I wanted to bury myself inside it.

My mouth was everywhere at once, all over her sweetness, lapping up the honey of her virgin pussy, nipping at her clit gently with my teeth, licking her in a steady rhythm over and over as I squeezed the base of my cock so I wouldn't come...

• • •

"Reece?" she asks, drawing me back to the moment.

Fuck.

I want to ask her a million questions. How did she find me? Why is she here? What does she want? But I'm unable to stop myself from studying her. Her skin looks so soft. I wonder if it's still lightly perfumed with lavender and honey. Long dark hair that flows over her shoulders, a trim waist, and the gentle curve of well-rounded hips. Dressed in skinny jeans, and tall boots, her shapely legs seem to go on forever.

She crosses her arms under her ample breasts bringing attention to the fact she has a glorious rack. Dear god. *Are those Ds?* "You've grown up," I say, recovering only slightly.

Noting how my eyes had briefly wandered from hers, Macey smirks. "So have you. Unless my memories are off. How tall are you these days?"

"Six-four."

"God, it's been a long time." She smiles at me, but there's a faraway sadness in her eyes I don't like.

"Six years," I say, even though it wasn't a question. "Does Hale know you're here?" Something tells me her older brother wouldn't be too happy she's shown up at my club.

Shaking her head, Macey tips her chin toward her chest.

Using two fingers, I lift her chin to meet my gaze. "Who's done this to you?"

"What?" she asks, flushed and slightly breathless.

That reaction is to be expected, given our surroundings. Crave is Chicago's hottest BDSM club. But her reaction to the club isn't what I'm referring to at all.

"Who's dimmed that light in your eyes?"

That was the thing about Macey. Even from the time she was a skinny little girl, those huge blue eyes were like two pools of light that swallowed you whole, sucked you into her orbit, and made you feel alive and slightly out of control.

I can't resist reaching out to touch her again, this time tucking a stray lock of chestnut-colored hair behind her ear. The urge to take her in my arms and hold her tight flares inside me. And to say I'm not the cuddling type would be a huge fucking understatement. But this is Macey, and I really don't like seeing her like this.

She inhales sharply at the contact, but her gaze stays on mine. "How about a drink first?"

I nod, and placing my hand against her lower back, lead the way toward the bar.

Helping Macey onto the only open bar stool, I stand beside her and gesture to the bartender.

My head is still spinning from the scene upstairs I just witnessed. I helped Hale with his new submissive, Brielle, just moment ago. She'd presented her tight little ass to us at his command, and even with her on display, all I could think about was getting back to Macey. I couldn't believe when my security staff called me over, pointing to the woman near the door who'd asked to speak with me. But before I could gather my courage to approach her, Hale called my cell, asking for backup with his scene. Of course I went.

All I could think about was Macey during the scene, how Hale's little fucking sister was out there waiting for me. If anyone tried to pick her up or take her to a private room, so help me, I would rip his arms off and beat him with them. And since that would be bad for business, I was hoping it didn't come to that. Hale would freak out if he knew she was here, so I kept things brief and stayed quiet about that fact, before slipping out of the room to return to her. And now that I'm standing with her, I'm speechless once again.

The bar is packed, given that it's New Year's, and we watch the bartender filling drink orders and slinging bottles for a couple of quiet moments.

"Why don't you start out by telling me exactly why you came here tonight?" I ask. Last I knew, Macey had been living in Miami.

"Let me give you a hint." She leans closer, letting the weight of her generous breasts brush against my chest as she bends close to my ear. "My personal life went to shit, and now I need hot, sweaty sex. I need forget-my-own-name sex."

The sweet little Macey I remember has left the building, folks.

My cock hardens instantly.

Just then, the bartender saunters up and asks what we're craving, a little tagline my publicity company came up with. All the bar staff and waitresses have been trained to use it.

Having not spent any time with the adult version of Macey, I have no idea what she drinks, so I'm surprised when she orders herself a whiskey, neat. It's a hell of a woman who drinks whiskey straight up, or maybe she's more thrown off at seeing me than she's letting on. I sure as fuck am. Something in me likes that she's not a fruity-drink type of girl. Her personality is straightforward and intoxicating, and her drink choice reflects it.

Once we've settled in with our cocktails, her eyes land on mine again. "So it's true then."

"What's true?" I ask before swallowing a mouthful of scotch.

"That you own this place."

I give her a nod.

She bites her lip as she toys with her glass, then brings her gaze back to me. "When I got into town tonight and Cameron wasn't answering his phone, I Googled you."

Watching her expression, I'm trying to read her, knowing she's thinking I never had a penchant for kink when she and I were together. But I'm not explaining the reason why to her. Now, or hopefully ever.

"How long will you be in town?" I ask, my curiosity edging out my better judgment.

"For good," she says, leveling me with those big blue eyes. "I lost my job, left my cheating ex-boyfriend, packed everything I owned, and here I am."

Damn.

Macey worked as a newscaster for a Latin TV station in Miami. She double-majored in Spanish and Journalism in college, earning both degrees ahead of schedule. She's smart and driven, and ambitious. Which is why it surprises me to hear her say she's just thrown in the towel on it all.

"I'm sorry to hear that." It explains the sadness radiating from her that I picked up on earlier. "So, what's on your agenda now, other than hot, sweaty pounding?"

"Why don't you finish that drink first, and I'll tell you."

"Are you trying to get me liquored up, Macey?"

"And what if I was?"

A slow, sassy smile uncurls on her mouth, and holy fuck. This girl is going be trouble; I can tell in an instant. But this can't be like six years ago where I lose my shit completely, only to have her waltz out of town again when the next opportunity pops up.

Acknowledgments

There are so many people to thank, the process is almost overwhelming, as is the fear that I'll inadvertently leave someone out.

My readers mean everything to me, and I'm blessed to have your support. I truly hope you enjoyed *The Gentleman Mentor*. It was one of those stories I wasn't planning on writing, but within a matter of hours, I could see how the whole book would play out. Brielle, and also Hale, who were both nameless for the first several days, were plotting together to embark on this arrangement, and I was all too happy to document their journey. At the moment, I'm deep into writing *Sinfully Mine* and enjoying every second of it. Where Brielle was unsure and timid, Macey is headstrong and opinionated. And Reece is a sexy dominant, so he's fun to write. I can't wait to share it with you.

To my friends and fellow authors, Meghan March and Rachel Brookes, your valuable insight always improves my writing. I'm grateful for you both.

To my dazzling publicist, Danielle Sanchez, your excitement over my work never gets old. I appreciate your partnership and guidance more than you'll ever know.

Pam Berehulke, it's an honor every time I'm able to work with you. I learn more each time, and I promise you, one of these days I'll get my pronoun usage under control. Pinky swear!

To all of the bloggers, fans, and readers who have shared my books with others, who've left reviews and made beautiful graphic teasers, my heart is filled with bookish love for you. I hope you know how critical you are to this community. I'm grateful for every tweet, review, and mention.

About the Author

Kendall Ryan is the *New York Times*, *USA TODAY*, and *Wall Street Journal* bestselling author of more than a dozen contemporary romance novels, including *Hard to Love*, *Resisting Her*, *When I Break*, and the Filthy Beautiful Lies series. Her books have been published into multiple languages and are sold in more than fifty countries around the world. She loves reading about tough alpha heroes with a sweet side, and aims to capture that in her writing. She detests laundry and enjoys coffee, cupcakes, and being outdoors playing with her two infant sons and darling husband.

Connect with Kendall Ryan

Website: www.kendallryanbooks.com

Facebook: Kendall Ryan Books

Twitter: @kendallryan1

Pinterest: www.pinterest.com/kendallryan1

Other Books by Kendall Ryan

When We Fall

When I Break (complete series)

FILTHY BEAUTIFUL LIES Series:

Filthy Beautiful Lies

Filthy Beautiful Love

Filthy Beautiful Lust

Filthy Beautiful Forever

Stand-alone Novels:

Hard to Love

Reckless Love

Resisting Her

The Impact of You

CPSIA information can be obtained
at www.ICGtesting.com
Printed in the USA
LVOW08s1824031017
551035LV00004B/768/P